AFRICAN WRITERS SERIES

Editorial Adviser · Chinua Achebe

12

THE AFRICAN

AFRICAN WRITERS SERIES

William Conton

THE AFRICAN

HEINEMANN

LONDON IBADAN NAIROBI

Heinemann Educational Books Ltd
48 Charles Street, London W1X 8AH
PMB 5205, Ibadan · POB 25080, Nairobi
EDINBURGH   MELBOURNE   TORONTO
AUCKLAND   HONG KONG   SINGAPORE
NEW DELHI

ISBN 0 435 90012 9

First published 1960 by William Heinemann Ltd
First published in *African Writers Series* 1964
Reprinted 1966, 1969, 1971

Printed in Malta by
St Paul's Press Ltd

TO BERTHA

CHAPTER ONE

M Y N A M E is Kisimi Kamara.

I was born at the height of a rainy season, in the village of
Lokko in the British West African colony of Songhai. My
father cultivated an acre of tired red soil round our hut and
fished a near-by muddy stream, wringing from these unimpressive resources a livelihood which most of the other
villagers regarded as enviable. I was the second son and the
fifth child in a family of eleven, and my childhood was consequently quite unspoilt. I have, since growing up, often
heard foreigners say that my people are a lazy, indolent folk.
Yet my earliest memories are of the incessant toiling of men
and women in and around our dusty compounds throughout the shimmering day, cooking, sweeping, building, dig-
ging, planting, harvesting. There were few enough moments
of relaxation for any grown-up before the sun went down,
and the long succession of babies which occupied my
mother's snug, sweaty back was lulled to sleep by the rhyth-
mic sound and movement which accompany the pounding
of rice. There was, it is true, a well-worn hammock hanging
from the veranda roof at the front of our hut; but we all
knew only too well how thoroughly well earned was every
swaying, creaking minute that our parents spent in it.

In addition to all her work in the house and compound,
my mother ran a palm-wine bar and a shop for the sale of
salt, groundnuts, and fresh fruit. Her counter was the low
mud wall of our front veranda, her till a cigarette tin; and
whenever business was good a few tins of provisions would
join the basin of salt and the fresh produce on the counter,
and the till would rattle merrily whenever she lifted it. We

1

lived right on the main road; and, it being the first house you came across as you entered the village, now and then a car or lorry would draw up to obtain water for a hissing radiator or for parched throats, or to buy some of my mother's goods. That was always a tremendous event for us children. We grew to tell quite a long way ahead, from the note of the engine, whether or not the driver was looking for somewhere to stop; and we would race out to inspect with solemn awe the wheezing machines we believed to be possessed of some mighty spirit, the conjuring up of which had been done in a distant land called Britain. The supercilious drivers who looked so knowingly under bonnets and chassis during the halt we thought of as a type of high priest, ministering to this spirit; and we would hand them a leaking kerosene tin of muddy well-water with almost as much reverence as a server passing the bishop the holy water. The dust-covered passengers, however, we somehow despised rather than envied; for they seemed so helpless and unhappy, whether they were in the first-class compartment beside the driver, or in the second-class behind.

In fact not one of us would have allowed himself to be carried a yard away from home in any mechanical contraption of any kind. Our world was then a supremely secure one; and we felt instinctively that those flying lorries, with their cloaks of red dust billowing behind them, came from another world that was not nearly so secure or safe; that they were in some way harbingers of evil. We never ventured so much as to climb on to a stationary lorry, even when the driver was out of his seat, for fear that we might be spirited away from our snug little *pied-à-terre*.

The village we all loved so well consisted of perhaps twenty mud houses grouped in compounds on either side of the main road. Each compound contained four or five houses arranged in a hollow square. One of these compounds, the biggest by far, was the chief's. His was the only house with corrugated iron roofing. Not even his wives' houses in the same compound had this luxury.

A little stream ran under the main road at one end of the village, near the school The bridge over this stream was only wide enough to take one car or lorry at a time. When we were having our twice-daily baths in the cool, clean water below, it was frightening to see how a lorry crossing the bridge leaned over, seeming always in danger of falling and crushing us.

I suppose I must at an early age have given some evidence of possessing better-than-average intelligence, for my family sent me to school – the only one of my brothers and sisters thus favoured. Perhaps, though, it was only that when we children squatted on the bare earth in front of the house, taking it in turns to invent stories, mine always seemed to be the lengthiest and most involved, as well as the most popular. But then my elder brother had learned to give my mother's customers their correct change at an earlier age than I, and one of my younger brothers could beat the drum much better than I could. I see now that, slight as were my father's contacts with the outside world, he had already learned that a high premium was set on a verbal dexterity in the big city on the coast (which, to the best of my knowledge, he only visited once), as well as in the great unknown world beyond, toward which that city turned its bemused face.

I do not remember ever hearing my father and mother discuss the question of my being sent to school. One morning, without any warning, my father said to me, 'Kisimi, put on your best gown, wash your feet, and follow me.' I must have been about ten years old at the time, for I was just tall enough to reach things on our veranda parapet from the ground outside. My father had put on his best khaki trousers and blue and white striped smock, and walked ahead of me down the two miles of road between our hut and the small school run

3

by American missionaries on the other side of the village.

We turned off the road up a neat gravelled path lined with short bushes of crimson double hibiscus set at regular intervals. To one side of the path was a dwarf-sized football field, and mango and avocado pear trees stood on the other side, the former with their blossoms, so much like Christmas-tree decorations, swaying softly in the breeze. My feelings as we stepped over the dusty threshold into the cool interior of the one-roomed school were compounded of curiosity and pride, but mainly of the latter. I knew virtually all the children in the school, and the difference in social standing between them and those of us who were not at school was not unlike that between the English public school pupil and his council school counterpart. Amongst us the important question was never 'How many palm trees does your father have?' or even 'Have you ever been to Sagresa?' but simply 'Do you go to school?'

The American lady who rose from her table in a corner of the room to greet us as we entered was, I thought, radiantly beautiful. She smiled as if she already knew and was very fond of us; her skin was white and red, and looked so soft and smooth that I longed to touch it. But when she spoke her voice sounded unmusical and unnatural, and even the little boy who was summoned to interpret for her seemed to have difficulty in understanding what she was saying. I marvel now at the speed with which we all learned to understand and speak the strange language she spoke, and to flatten our intonation as she did.

And so to school. At the cost only of having to do without my help in the house and yard (we paid no school fees), my parents started me off that day on the long, endless road of schooling; a road on which, for me, every milestone was to be a signpost pointing ahead, and every step of the way a sharpener of the intellectual appetite. It was in that dusty school compound, amongst the hibiscus and mangoes, and

4

in the cool of the schoolroom, straining to catch the meaning of the words spoken by the smiling white lady, that I first caught a glimpse of a prospect that was almost intolerably exciting and attractive. I know now that it was attractive only because it was then entirely strange, and largely misunderstood by us all, not least by our teachers.

Most of us learned very quickly. We forced ourselves to speak English whenever possible. We memorised avidly the spelling and meaning of every word in the small hymnbooks which were at first our sole and highly prized schoolbooks. We would stay on for hours after school testing each other at the blackboard on the letters of the alphabet, on numerals, on spelling, and later on grammar. When Miss Schwartz announced in school one day that she wanted one of us to come and live with her, to help her with domestic duties outside school hours, there was a rush to volunteer which took her completely by surprise. When she had recovered and had quieted our excited shouting and bid us lower the forest of stretching arms, there was a moment during which none of us dared breathe, as she scanned the eager faces. What made her choose me I have never found out, but I had noticed before that she was partial toward me, as children always do notice such things soon enough.

'All right, Kisimi. You can come. But run along and ask your father first, and remember you will only stay with me as long as you are a good boy.'

I imagine my parents were only too glad to have one mouth fewer to feed, and my brothers and sisters to see the back of one who, inevitably, had begun to assume an air of learned superiority in talking to them. Miss Schwartz's bungalow was a stone's throw from the school, and that very evening saw me installed on a mat in a corner of her back veranda, unable to sleep with excitement at the thought of the good fortune that had befallen me. To be within earshot of Miss Schwartz's English all day, to have access (I hoped) to her books, to nurse the possibility, overwhelming even in thought, of going with her to Sagresa and perhaps even further away; all these visions kept my eyes wide open and my brain racing until very late that night. With my cloth pulled right over my head to keep the mosquitoes away, warm and snug in my own cocoon, happy beyond all description in my heart, I smiled myself to sleep.

I learned a very great deal in Miss Schwartz's bungalow, apart from improving my English beyond my wildest hopes. I learned much about the world outside, and began to sense that there were barriers much higher and much less easily gauged than those of mere language and colour, between the people amongst whom I was born and those from whom she sprang. The smiling teacher in the daytime often became the brooding, restless, cross-tempered missionary in the evenings. Her bungalow was shared by another young missionary, a doctor, also American, who was in charge of a small clinic in the next village, and who travelled backward and forward between the two villages on a bicycle. I noticed that when not at their work or talking about it these two women gave far fewer signs of being happy than did my own womenfolk at home. As I grew up with them I found myself wondering what had made them leave their own lands and come to live this strange life amongst a people whose ways were so totally different from their own.

Young as I then was, I noticed that these two women very seldom relaxed entirely, or behaved in the easy and natural manner to which I was used among my own people. Their conversation with each other and with us, their very smiles, as I came to realise before long, were artificial and assumed. Among the few occasions when I sensed that they were experiencing deep emotion, which they could not or would not attempt to stifle, were the daily prayer meetings, and the visits to the bungalow of the new Assistant District Commissioner.

The prayer meetings were, of course, compulsory for me – not that I needed much persuading to attend regularly, for I was determined to seize every opportunity of enlarging my English vocabulary, even if only by listening to devotional language of decidedly Quakerish complexion. But as Miss Schwartz and Miss Costello poured out their souls to God in that kerosene-lit living-room, with a fervent concentration which fascinated me, I knew that somewhere behind those passionate moments lay the answer to my question as to their purpose in coming here at all. They seemed at such times to be able to forget the present altogether; and it was only much later in life that I realised that it was the past, as much as anything, which they were both trying so hard to forget. Their faces would light up with a sublime, almost ecstatic contentment, words would flow in a ceaseless stream from their lips; and often, my own etymological and phonetic interest in their outpourings forgotten, I would be caught up in the spirit of their devotions, and, in my turn, pray almost as eloquently in my own language as they had done in theirs. 'God bless you, Kisimi,' they would exclaim gratefully.

The Assistant District Commissioner's visits were to provide relaxation of quite another kind. These visits began soon after I joined the household. I well remember the first one. My guardians had been given no warning of it, it seemed; for they were at supper (with me as apprentice steward) when the sound of a car stopping on the road made them start – a rare enough occurrence it was in those days. A tall, bronzed, sun-helmeted figure emerged from the car, surveyed the compound with a monarch-of-all-I-survey expression, and then strode purposefully up the path. In a trice both women had disappeared into their bedrooms, in more of a hurry and in greater discomfiture than I had ever seen them. I was left to show the visitor to a seat, and to assure him, in a laboured admixture of English, Hausa, and gesturing, that the ladies he wished to see were in.

7

After a while they emerged, and to my surprise I noticed that they had spent the interval in changing their dresses and rearranging their hair. They seemed awkward, even gawky in manner, and to my chagrin I could now follow hardly any of their conversation. I was only aware that it was much less voluble than their prayers, and that they appeared much better able to control their feelings now than when they were on their knees.

After a short while their visitor rose to go, politely refusing the drink which they only then remembered to offer him, and was accelerating away in front of a cloud of dust a minute or two later. I noticed that my guardians both watched from behind the curtains until the dust had settled, and although their feeling of relief at his departure was unmistakable, the colour in their cheeks seemed a little higher than usual. During the remainder of that meal their usual taciturnity was replaced by a continuous flow of conversation in which the name 'Mr Anderson' recurred constantly.

Mr Anderson, a handsome Scot, out on his first tour, soon became the most regular of their very infrequent visitors; and he grew to be so thoroughly at ease in that bungalow that, a few weeks later, far from being offered a drink only when he rose to go, he was soon helping himself unbidden at the sideboard. That item of furniture was, of course, kept strictly undefiled by any suggestion of alcohol, even such slight suggestion as might have been contained in a gourd of fresh palm-wine. Many years later, when I asked a then somewhat mellowed Mr Anderson what he had found of interest in these visits to the missionary bungalow, he gave me a most entertaining account of the last of those visits. I have no doubt that this story derived quite as much from his imagination as from his memory; but if it is even only a quarter true, it is worth relating here as showing how welcome to missionaries and colonial officials alike is any diversion that will relieve the tedium of life out on a lonely station.

According to him, then, after perhaps a dozen of his informal calls at their bungalow, the two women had ceased to disguise the pleasure they found in his company, and increasingly to forget the difference, as he put it, between his post-mortem destination and their own. He in his turn took an innocent delight in ferreting out from them details of their private lives. He succeeded in discovering that they had both received their call to convert African pagans soon after having been jilted, whilst still at high school, by a pair of young American pagans 'back home'; at which news he claims he made a series of cluck-clucking noises, which successfully conveyed commiseration. The more the conversation had grown entertaining, however, the more he had regretted the total absence of any civilised liquid refreshment to go with it. At one point he did pluck up enough courage to remark that life in the tropics could appear vastly enhanced when viewed through a glass of gin and lime; but the remark was not well received. His hostesses had spent a full minute contemplating their mosquito boots in embarrassment, at the end of which period the doctor had said with exaggerated brightness: 'Lime is wonderful for preventing scurvy, isn't it?'

It was at that moment, if he is to be believed, that Mr Anderson swore to get gin fumes into their breath or perish in the attempt. On his next visit to the bungalow a small bottle of Gordon's disturbed ever so slightly the smooth line of one of his mosquito boots, and at a suitable moment a drop or two of its contents were introduced into the glasses he was pouring out at the sideboard. Throughout the evening he increased the dosage, at the same time increasing the strength of the lime to disguise the taste. He achieved so much success in this delicate operation that, apart from observing that Rose's seemed to be getting their lime from

9

quite a different plantation these days, neither of his victims suspected anything. Soon he was able to try out his favourite joke about the Scottish parson who used to cut up his stale crusts into small pieces, some for his canaries and some for his communicants; and when this irreverent sally was greeted with shrill girlish laughter he felt satisfied. I apparently looked around the edge of the veranda in alarm at the sound of this unaccustomed raucousness.

'Hi, Jo! Wha-do-you-know?' asked Miss Schwartz of me.

'Amen, so let it be,' put in Miss Costello with a loud belch.

And I retreated quickly, mystified and mortified. What happened next Mr Anderson would never reveal. Some hours later, he claimed, both ladies were fast asleep in their chairs; he had thoughtfully thrown blankets over them to protect them from the harmattan; smelled their reeking breath contentedly; and walked out, triumphant if a little unsteady, to his car.

That, Jim Anderson added rather unnecessarily, was the last such visit. The following day a massive figure which he recognised as the superintendent of the mission sparred her way up his drive, and he had to take hasty and silent refuge for a whole hour in the outhouse which served as his toilet, before she left. She must have been a determined woman, however; for she sparred her way up several other drives to such effect that a month later he was summoned to the Chief Secretary's offices in Sagresa, rapped severely over the knuckles, and transferred to another district.

I cannot recollect the incident at all. I do remember however that Mr Anderson's visits to the bungalow ceased very suddenly, to my great regret, for he represented for me at that time one more source of English words. Nevertheless I made such good progress at all the subjects available in the missionary school that, after a few years (I do not know exactly how many), I was pronounced by my teachers ready for secondary school.

CHAPTER TWO

THE CAPITAL, Sagresa, meant to me a new and exciting world I knew about only from the glowing accounts of it brought back by my lorry-driver friends, and the somewhat less flattering remarks dropped about it by my guardians. But to my parents it meant mainly sending me into the midst of a people whom I soon realised they regarded with deep mistrust. The people of the coast, they would tell me, had been mixing with white men so much that, in spite of their black skins, they had become foreigners in their language and customs. There were dark hints that the Sagresans had deprived us of some of our land, and on occasions joined the white man in fighting against us. Older folk in our village remembered one occasion when, it was said, the white man and his coastal friends had gone a little too far in bullying us and lording it over us. There had been a big rising of our people, which resulted in many deaths, and did nothing to improve relations between us and the 'black foreigners'.

On the other hand, to send me to a town other than Sagresa for my secondary schooling, we all realised, would deprive me of an excellent opportunity to discover the world outside the narrow limits in which I had been brought up, and particularly of the mysterious white man's world. With that sure instinct which the untutored so often display, my father was seeking for me an education liberal rather than conservative, exploratory rather than traditional.

So in the end to Sagresa I went. My last days in Lokko are days that stand out with vivid clarity in my memory. As I went backward and forward for the last time between the bungalow where I had learned so much during the past four years and the home which housed my undisguisedly envious brothers and sisters, it seemed that scales had fallen from my eyes, and that I was seeing for the first time the real beauty of the natural scenery amongst which I had lived all these years. The green carpet of foliage on the slopes across the road from our hut had never looked so soft in shade and so even and unruffled in texture as now. A giant acalypha bush near our front door was aflame, its broad red leaves richly burnished. At the missionary bungalow a scarlet bougainvillaea plant which among others, it had been my pleasant duty to tend, had just reached the roof, and was throwing a blossom-laden strand curling back on itself over the entrance. Even the cluster of banana trees down by the side of the road appeared to make up, in the graceful movement of their broad fronds in the breeze, what they lost of beauty through wearing incessantly a thick covering of red dust thrown up by the flying lorries. The monkeys playing in the young mango trees, so often the targets for our stones, seemed now to be cocking their heads at me with a new interest, as if they too had heard that I had been singled out for special favours. I winked at them affectionately, and one old grandfather among them appeared to me to wink back quite slowly and deliberately, as if to assure me that they harboured no ill-feelings against me for deserting them.

It was in my mother, however, that I suddenly noticed most that was new. I had always taken her for granted, assumed that all she gave to me was my right to have and her duty to give. I was vaguely aware that she worked herself to exhaustion for her children. But it was only now, as my separation from her drew near, that I realised how good and fair she was. Like all my father's wives, my mother was a much more real and approachable figure to her children than was my father. We saw very little of our father, and perhaps as a result took him for granted less.

A good and fair mother. She was still quite young then,

tall, slim, with an ebony-smooth skin, so beautiful and black it almost looked steel-blue in moonlight. Her breasts were still round and firm, and it was her feet and hands which really showed what she had given her children. Her feet were already splayed out from much walking under heavy loads, and her hands chapped and calloused. But to me now she appeared more than ever the fairest and best of mothers.

The plan was that the mission, which had come to regard me as one of its showpiece pupils, should be responsible for meeting the whole cost of my secondary schooling in Sagresa. I would continue in a missionary household in the capital the mutually profitable arrangement of doing household chores after school hours in exchange for free board and lodging, and my parents would be charged only with the duty of keeping me decently clothed and supplied with pocket money. The business fortunes of both my parents had risen, my father having done so well at his fishing and farming that he now enjoyed the income from a flock of about thirty sheep and one and a half scattered acres of upland rice. My mother's trading had outgrown our front veranda, and was housed in a ramshackle shed of its own in the front patch of garden. It was not difficult for them, consequently, to undertake these limited financial responsibilities on my behalf, and, indeed, I am quite sure that they would gladly have undertaken much more had it proved to be necessary.

It was a very wet day at the beginning of the rainy season when my father, Miss Schwartz (who had recently returned from furlough in the United States) and I climbed aboard the lorry which was to take me on my first journey away from the village where I was born and which had thus far contained my entire experience of life. My friends and relatives all gathered to see me off, and my mother's eyes shone with pride and her voice shrilled with excitement as she and my father enlarged to the company on the future they saw ahead for me. Strong muscles glistened in the driving rain. I manoeuvred my solitary soap box of luggage into such a position on the floor of the crowded lorry as would enable my father to sit on it in relative dryness and comfort during the journey, and then squatted on the tailboard to exchange final farewells with the chattering group on the muddy road-side. I suddenly realised to what extent I had now become the focus of the hopes and ambitions of practically everyone in my village. There was now more than mere envy of my good fortune. In my departure for secondary schooling in Sagresa, Lokko saw both a recognition of its own growing importance, and an opportunity to accelerate still further that growth. More, much more, than good wishes were going with me. Everything that could be done by way of ritual and ceremony, to assure the success of the venture on which I was now launching, had been done. If some of the ritual was non-Christian, this was my people's way of splitting the risks.

The lorry driver and his numerous assistants finished their ministrations under the bonnet, and the engine sprang suddenly, noisily, and smokily to life. Feeling very far from tears, and elated with excitement, I saw Miss Schwartz put her head round the side of the driver's cab (she was travelling first-class). I heard her say, with a smile almost as pleased and happy as mine must have been, 'You're on your way, Tom Brown!' My father and I exchanged final shouted remarks with the others on the road, the gears grated, the lorry lurched and lumbered wheezily off; and distance, dust, and exhaust smoke soon swallowed up the little group which to me represented home, love, security.

I do not remember very much about the journey itself, except that at one point the road ran parallel to a railway line for a few hundred yards, and, to my great delight, I caught my first glimpse of a train. My first sight of the snorting, spark-ing, clanking engine and its short crocodile of swaying carriages whistling along the shining track was a token of wonders yet to come. I must have gaped and goggled at it quite unrestrainedly; for my interest in it provoked a stream of information, most of which I later found completely inaccurate, about railways and how they worked. Then suddenly the rattling and bouncing ceased, the red road turned black, and the lorry shook off its cloak of dust. It ran humming along now, down a steep slope to a little bridge across a stream; and then up the other side of the gorge. Halfway up, the note of its engine, which had gradually been dropping down the scale, coughed out, brakes were hastily applied, and we all had to get out and walk up the rest of the slope, while our vehicle dragged its lightened bulk up in front of us. At the top we clambered aboard again and resumed our journey; and soon afterwards the closing gap between the enormous houses which receded from my view, told me that we were entering the capital. In a few minutes we were outside the mission house, and I was forced to give all my attention to the task of unloading Miss Schwartz's luggage, my father's, and my own.

I was soon an interested bystander at an interpreted interview between my father and the general superintendent of the mission. I learned that I was to be prepared during the course of the next few months to sit the entrance examination to one of the secondary schools in Sagresa. If successful, as everyone seemed confident I would be, I was to enter the school as a boarder. My father appeared to be highly satisfied with these plans. He thanked the missionary profusely for his kindness, presenting him with the gifts we had brought down specially from our village for this moment – an enclosed basket containing three live fowls, and an open one containing a generous and varied collection of fresh fruit. These gifts were received with a warmth of gratitude to match my father's; and we were then shown the cupboard under the staircase where I was to sleep and keep all my belongings (a considerable improvement, I realised at once, on the open veranda corner I had used in the missionary bungalow at Lokko). Having bundled my sleeping mat and my box into my snug little boudoir, I went out with my father to have my first good look at Sagresa.

My recollection of that first walk through those crowded streets is confused. One or two impressions persist – of large numbers of people in the markets, most of them speaking a language which was neither English nor Hausa. The houses were mostly made of stone or wood, many of them appearing to have a kind of enclosed veranda running along the front of the first floor. There appeared to be a fair number of white faces to be seen behind the counters of shops and the windscreens of cars. I had not yet learned to distinguish between the Syrian and the European white faces, so I was much impressed at the enlarged opportunities I imagined I would now have of listening to and learning good English – to me then the very purpose of existence.

Then there was the sea. As to any schoolboy anywhere, people and the works of people's hands were of more immediate interest and concern to me than the works of nature. But my first glimpse of the sea at the end of one of the streets leading to the harbour filled me with awe and wonder. I had seen nothing in the way of natural scenery other than the landscape around my village. But I knew at once that this was something romantic and unordinary, and that it would win my heart. Throughout the years since, I have heard travellers to West Africa, usually disgruntled servicemen who had the misfortune of being casseroled in a troopship in a harbour for days on end, refer only to the heat of this loveliest of coasts. But their view is understandably jaundiced; for to judge fairly it is necessary to put oneself to the trouble of going ashore and getting away from the town, away to the hills and to the villages, whose quiet, unhurried charm would escape only the most insensitive of souls. Then one needs to go down to the coves and beaches where the surf creams endlessly and the cocoanut palms droop trembling fronds from arching stems.

But these were later discoveries. For the present the wideness of the sea and the greenness of the sloping land filled my eyes; and as I curled up that night outside the entrance to my cupboard (which my father was occupying for the night) they also filled the background of my dreams. And the sky which roofed them over contained no cloud that my young eyes could see.

Next day I said good-bye to my father and watched the lorry carry him away, with a lot of noisy hooting, down narrow Prince Henry Street and away toward the long brown dusty road. I suddenly realised as the lorry disappeared round a corner that that road was now my only visible link with my village. I felt more exhilarated than anything else at the thought. Rather than return to the mission house immediately, I decided to take advantage of this new and stimulating sense of personal freedom by exploring Sagresa and its vicinity on my own.

I first discovered a vast building with thick walls on the shore, and guessed from the soldiers standing at the gates in uniforms of storybook splendour that this was where the Governor himself must live. I went as close as I dared to the forbidding cannon guarding the walls, approached one of the sentries, and looked admiringly at the shining rifle he carried. I had read a lot about guns, and had seen many homemade hunting guns in the village. I thought, disappointedly, that his looked decorative and unbusinesslike. Something in the sentry's face prompted me to speak to him in Hausa; and, to my great delight, I found he was of my tribe. Without moving his head or body, and in low undertones, he asked me what village I was from, and what I was doing alone so far from home; and in return he answered my eager questions. Had he ever fought in a war? – No. Had any of the other soldiers? – No. Were many of them

Hausas? – Yes, most of them were Hausa-speaking. Could I come and talk to him and the others now and then? – Yes, but only when they were off duty.

And with that I had to be content. But my pleasure at finding one of my own people in what was for me a completely new world was proof that, below, all my excitement, nostalgia and homesickness were merely lying dormant, awaiting a convenient opportunity to assert themselves. Later, of course, I found many others of my tongue in Sagresa, but the Governor's soldiers never lost their place in my affections as both my first heroes and my first friends, in a town big and strange and altogether different from anything I had known before.

I continued my ramble up to the top of a small hill, to find there only a repulsively ugly row of buildings apparently full of soldiers or policemen – I could not tell which. The view, however, was superbly dramatic – acre upon acre of roofs, some rusty-brown, others red or green, set among tall trees of every kind – breadfruit, mango, palm, frangipani, flamboyants, under a blazing sky. And, unchallenged king of the trees, stood the great cotton tree which I already knew had sent its wispy white flakes drifting down over so much of Sagresa's history. It now seemed to have the magnetic power of drawing the gaze of people in whatever quarter of the town they might be. Then down to a high cliff near the harbour, from which I obtained my first view of an ocean-going ship. One was just steaming in, standing high in the water, black smoke belching from her funnel, and white water churning under her stern. She moved infinitely slowly to her anchorage. I watched with increasing reverence the white man's magic, as the anchor chain rattled downward with a rumble which reached me quite clearly where I stood, and the surf boats and other small craft fussed out to cluster around her like so many ducklings round their mother. Imperious siren blasts, issuing from under a plume of white steam, summoned more attendant craft, and clearly brooked no delay. As I turned away I determined that, God willing, I too should sail in one of those ships and obtain from those lands across the seas whatever it was they might have to offer me of knowledge, of skill, and of power.

The first person I saw as I re-entered the back compound of the mission house was my father. His lorry had skidded into a tree when one of the tyres had blown out. The terrified but unhurt driver had promptly abandoned his vehicle and passengers to their fate and disappeared into the bush. There being no other driver amongst the passengers, they had all had to make their way back to town as best they could. My father had been able to stop and board another lorry travelling to Sagresa. Since it was too late by then to expect to obtain long-distance transport out of town, he would be forced to keep me out of my cupboard for another night, he said.

It was the first time my father had ever suggested that my giving up any of my comfort or sacrificing my convenience for him was a matter even worthy of comment, and I saw that a new relationship was beginning to develop between us. Hitherto, contact between my father and myself had been of the very slightest. We might not exchange words for days on end, except for the orders he would give me whilst I was working, and it was my mother to whom I had been trained to look for parental guidance and tutelage. The fact that my father had more children than my mother only partly accounted for this difference in relationship. I fancy it was also partly due to the inherited tradition amongst our menfolk that, until such time as the Dapo secret society had performed its task of turning the boy into the man, the distinction between the two must not be blurred by unnecessary contact. When I went into the Dapo groves later I began to appreciate the wisdom of this view.

That second evening in Sagresa, however, which my father

and I were spending together more by chance than anything else, I felt that he came nearer to carrying on a conversation with me than he had ever done before. The mission house cook, who had been instructed to make sure we were fed after the missionaries had had their supper, spoke Hausa; so we three sat together under the stars in one corner of the back compound after supper and talked – or at least the two men talked and I listened, for the most part. But now and again my father would ask me a question as to how I felt about being in Sagresa alone, or about my studies; and I knew that back at home my presence would not have been tolerated in the company of my father and another adult, much less would my talking have been encouraged.

It was that quiet conversation that brought home to me more strongly than anything else could have done, I suppose, the great changes which this launching out of mine was going to effect in my home. I realised, with feelings of embarrassment that already, before even entering secondary school, I had learned much more than either of my parents ever had or would; and that this fact, which might appear now superficially to be closing the gap between my father and me, was in fact widening it in every important respect. Young as I was, I could see this with absolute clarity; and the sight of it, and the pain which accompanied it, brought to my eyes the first tears I had shed for years. I did not want things to change; I had been supremely happy with things as they were, and dreaded any new developments in my home life. But I could also see clearly that I could not have things both ways, that a choice had to be made, and in fact already had been. The thought of turning back now never seriously entered my head. But I will not deny that on that second evening in Sagresa, squatting on the hard-baked mud floor of that missionary compound, I experienced for the first time chilling misgivings as to what the future really held in store for me.

Next day my father succeeded in leaving Sagresa. We had a three-hour wait in the lorry before the driver could collect a pay-load of passengers; but at least it was a relief to be assured that the driver was this time also the owner of the vehicle, and would consequently be less likely to abandon it with the alacrity the other had displayed. There was, in fact, no mishap this time; and in due course a verbal message was delivered to me in Sagresa from my father, confirming his safe return.

The months between my arrival in Sagresa and my sitting the entrance examination to my secondary school were ones of unremitting hard work. I was coached intensively for the examination in a manner which would thoroughly disgust the modern educational theorist. Ill-advised or not, the coaching was certainly effective, and I passed the examination easily enough. When my father received my message informing him of my success, he sent me a letter which I have always treasured, not only as the first letter I ever received, but also as something which for many years afterward served as a spur to my ambitions and a strengthener of my determination to make good. Written in the small, careful hand of a teacher at my old school who doubled as our village letter-writer, the letter first brought me the congatulations of my father and all my family on my success. Then my father went on to remind me that I had now started to climb a palm tree which was high and difficult to climb; that many were watching my progress, and much ripe fruit was awaiting me on the successful conclusion of my climb. He ended with the warning that if I failed to reach the top, those watching me, both living and dead, would curse me for failing them. On the other hand, if I reached the top in order simply to gorge myself with fruit, I would surely become sick and fall to the ground and die. But if I returned to my people to share with them the fruit of my labours, then all would sing to my praise and thank me and honour those who had brought me to life.

Before receiving that letter, homesickness and a general sense of loss of security had made miserable the moments when I was not engaged in my lessons or my reading. I knew that I wanted to pass this examination; but beyond that I was not really sure of the direction in which I was travelling, or of the purposes which were to be achieved. But my father's first letter to me gave me an aim and an objective, and helped me to forget my misgivings. To know that my whole people would not hesitate to reject and scorn my success if it were not applied to their advancement, this was the link I was searching for between the happy security I had known in the past, and the half-seen promise which lay ahead of me now.

CHAPTER THREE

MY NEW SCHOOL was housed in a building which had been in turn a private house, a paupers' home, and a prison. Had we known at the time about all those interesting phases of the building's history, we might have invented a number of suitable jokes about it. But we did not; so we merely regarded the ungainly, thick-walled structure with a deep affection and reverence. It was large, as Sagresa buildings went then, standing in its own unpaved yard. The ground floor was a few feet below the level of the surrounding yard and the middle floor consisted of a big room which could be divided up by movable partitions into a variety of shapes for use as classrooms. The dormitories were on the top floor. At least three times as many rats as boys slept on that floor; but in due course the two parties achieved a state of peaceful co-existence. Housemasters also shared our accommodation under the corrugated roof, whilst the principal and his family lived in a house built onto the main school building, and which also contained the chapel and the school printing press.

By English standards I suppose, and even by Sagresan standards, I would have been regarded as old to start a secondary education, for I must have been sixteen or seventeen at the time. By English standards, too, we would all have been considered 'swots'. We worked hard, without exception; for those who did not received short shrift from the masters. A ruler across the knuckles was the immediate penalty for obtuseness in class, and expulsion for bringing up the rear in the form order. Our basic fare included Greek (which we all loved) and mathematics, and these two subjects were also those in excelling at which we took the greatest pride. We saw very little of the principal except in chapel, and what we saw of him made us take good care not to see more. He was tall and thin and possessed a vulture-beak nose. A punitive summons to his office was invariably followed by two or three days in the sick bay, tossing vainly to prevent raw buttocks from coming into contact with anything.

I was, for my first two years at the school, the only Hausa-speaking boy in my form, although there were several others in other forms. At first, there is no denying, my Sagresan classmates regarded me as their inferior, and my Sagresan roommates as an uncultured intruder who needed civilising. I cannot tell where I found the good sense to take all this in good part; but I learned somehow to rely on my conviction that sooner or later I should prove my worth by my own efforts, and wring from all concerned full acceptance as an equal. I learned, painfully, to smile the smile of unruffled composure when the language in classroom or dormitory changed, in my presence, from English to Sagresan and I sensed that I was its subject. This pretence became unnecessary after the end of the first year, for by then I could understand and speak Sagresan perfectly, and give as good as I got.

But I believe that it was not only my capacity for taking a joke against myself and my people which led to my rapid acceptance in that schoolboy society – and perhaps not even mainly this. The two achievements which I soon found commanded most respect in the school were success in classwork, and having the funds to dress like a sporting young toff. The first requirement I did not find it difficult to meet, as I was soon at the top of the form. As for the second, it was fortunate for my reputation at school that my parents' livelihood was constantly improving, and I was always able to hold my own when it came to dressing in the style considered elegant amongst us then. Trouser turn-ups were beneath notice if they measured less than a foot in width or less than

24

two inches in depth. An Edwardian touch came in with the straw boaters, which were part of the formal school uniform, and, when rained upon, sagged limply like wet socks around our ears.

Very little importance was attached to games and sports at that time, fortunately for me; for I was exceedingly maladroit at most activities of that nature. We were occasionally required to go out cross-country running, proceeding down a rocky slope near the school, through the shallow waters of a creek, up the other side, and around a peninsula. We all had to turn out for this, including the lame, halt and blind, so the pace was not hot; and the only harm done was the whetting of appetites which school food, like school food everywhere, usually failed to satisfy.

In view of my later experiences of inter-tribal dissensions in Africa, this early proof of the unifying effect of common objects, a common education, and shared living, on divergent origins and tribal backgrounds, was to be of the utmost importance to me. After that first term there was nothing in my speech or the cut of my clothes (as there had never been anything in the colour of my skin or in my physical features) to distinguish me from any other boy in the lower school; and, my name apart, no one, however observant, could in the second term have picked me out as not being a Sagresan.

Thus the Sagresan boys – and their parents – accepted me fully into their society soon enough. The girls were, however, a somewhat tougher proposition. I remember walking down Prince Henry Street one evening during my second year at the school, in company with one of the seniors from the North. I had at that time not yet developed much more than a whistling interest in girls, being then still conscious of my need to put in extra work, especially at English, in order to make up for the late start I had had as compared with my classmates. My friend Kodjo, however, was older and not

25

quite so ingenuous as I was; moreover he said he thought he knew one of the two girls who, in their starched school uniforms, were strolling ahead of us. We quickened our pace until we were walking, silently, a step or two behind them. Kodjo swore later that they had seen the pursuit out of the corner of their eyes and had obligingly slowed down. I cannot vouch for this. I do know that at that moment Kodjo allowed the excitement of the moment to get the better of him, and spoke to me in Hausa. The effect was immediate. Without even looking round at us, the ladies indulged in a contemptuous and prolonged sucking of the teeth, and quickened their steps to a pace which even Kodjo felt it imprudent to match.

This incident hurt nothing in me but my pride. For it was not until the school holidays immediately following it that I was sent by my parents in Dapo. Membership of any secret society was strictly forbidden by the mission which was educating me; and the missionaries believed at the time that I was merely going home for my first visit to my parents since coming to Sagresa. It was ironical, I have often thought since, that it was necessary for me to come to Sagresa in order to be able to enter Dapo. Such a subterfuge would have been impossible had I remained under the close surveillance of Miss Schwartz and Miss Costello in the missionary bungalow in Lokko.

So I entered a hothouse in which, for six weeks, the pace of my physical and mental development from boyhood into manhood was deliberately quickened. This was done so effectively that I entered the society's groves a child and emerged an adult. My sisters all underwent a similar preparation for adulthood in Dopo, the female secret society. The English girl becomes a woman the day she puts on her first brassiere, the Songhaian the day she graduates from this society.

As for the boys, we were trained to become skilful soldiers,

husbands and fathers. Many other highly disciplined appren-
ticeships were served, so that we might play our parts worthily
as custodians of the tribe's physical and cultural heritage.
We were taught to drum, to sing, and to dance. We learned
the tribe's history and its store of folk tales and proverbs.
We were shown the way to its sacred shrines and relics.
Above all, we were made to swear eternal loyalty to all our
brothers and sisters in the tribe, and to our ancestors and
gods.

Back to school from Lokko and Dapo, and to four more
years of single-minded study. I found now that time was
racing by fleet-footed, and the School Certificate Examination which, to every secondary school child in British Africa,
appeared then the supreme challenge to human endeavour,
drew quickly nearer. During my last year in school I worked
at my books at least ten hours a day. The picture I kept in
my mind's eye was the one my father's first letter to me had
evoked. I was making progress up my palm tree. The anxious
eyes were watching me from below, the patient prize awaited
me above – to be shared, not gorged. If I looked elsewhere
than at what I was doing the disaster which would result
would be widespread. So I gave myself completely to the task
in hand. When my parents sent me pocket money, I would
save as much as I could to pay for extra coaching in the subjects in which I was weakest. I mixed with as many pupils
from other secondary schools as I could, not for the sake of
their company, but in order to discover from them who were
the best teachers in their schools. Then, unbeknown to my
own teachers, I would make private arrangements for such
coaching as I felt I needed. This all meant extra homework
and added strain, but I learned to gauge nicely each day just
how far my brain could be driven, and to stop work in good
time. My sole recreation during this period was walking in
the hills and swimming at the beaches; and I trained myself
to relax completely and banish from my mind all thoughts

connected with my studies whilst I was away from my books. I had many friends now, and could always find company for my outings when I wanted it.

The truth was that, far from my being alone in my obsession with preparing for this examination, almost every other candidate for it was devoting a similar amount of time and energy to such preparation. It is impossible for anyone who has not been a pupil in a secondary school in Africa to visualise just what the School Certificate Examination means to us. If you pass it, not only will you be able to secure relatively well-paid employment almost immediately in business or the civil service, but you will be admitted to the select ranks of the 'educated minority', the 'intelligentsia', who are the pride and joy of their relatives and friends and the despair of the Colonel Blimps of British imperialism. We were all fully conscious of this, and the determination to satisfy the exacting requirements of the examining bodies of the University of Cambridge became an all-consuming passion. In spite of all the advice we received to the contrary from teachers and parents, most of us burned a large volume of midnight oil at our studies. Our hurricane lamps became amongst our most prized possessions, secreted away during the day in all kinds of odd corners against discovery by housemasters, parents or guardians. I have often wondered since how we escaped doing permanent injury to our eyesight by this practice, particularly as so much of our 'studying' consisted in reading over and over again sentences and formulae until we had committed them to memory.

It was during my final year at secondary school that I first developed the interest in politics which was later on to be the supreme influence in shaping the course of my life. I was secretary of the school Debating Society, and, with our usual love of long and erudite-sounding words, we had framed a motion for debate one week which promised good sport – 'That municipal government in this town is democratic in form and gerontocratic in fact.' We had often laughed amongst ourselves at the ripe old average age of councillors, aldermen and all others in positions of authority or influence in Sagresa; and one of our stock jokes was that amongst the requirements for any sort of promotion to high municipal office was to hold the School Certificate and to be long in the tooth. The motion was proposed by the only municipal councillor we had been able to find who was under forty, and was seconded by the senior prefect of the school. To oppose it we invited a seventy-three-year-old alderman, who had as his seconder the oldest pupil in the school (a fifth-former who was the proud possessor of a birth certificate which was carefully kept out of sight of the principal and the staff, since it revealed his age as twenty-seven; and whose son was rumoured to bring him a packed lunch to school every day).

The president of the Debating Society and I had had considerable difficulty in persuading the councillor and alderman to take part in the debate at all; and the whole school had been warned beforehand both by the principal and by the senior prefect that due regard must be paid to the status of the two guest speakers, and that there was to be no attacking of municipal greybeards generally. The warning was heeded, and our guests were heard with deference. Perhaps the warning was unnecessary, for Africans generally have a deep and ingrained respect for old age, and even when we can find nothing to admire in an old man, we will not easily forget that his grey hairs have earned him the right to courtesy and politeness. So all the heckling was reserved for our own twenty-seven-year-old. Shouts of 'Methuselah' and 'Grandpa', and attempts to put a walking stick in his hand and a pair of spectacles on his nose, punctuated his speech, and entirely destroyed the effects of any eloquence he might have been producing. He was, however, a good sport, and took it all in excellent spirit. (Later on he was to become the object of admiring envy to many hundreds of schoolchildren in Sagresa by walking off with a Grade I School Certificate.)

But for me the significance of that debate lay not in the eminence of our guest speakers or the thick skin of 'Grandpa', but in the sad truth which, as we all knew well enough, the motion contained. As I sat taking notes of the speeches, I wondered again and again whether it was really necessary to live so long before one was qualified to make a useful contribution to public affairs in one's town or village. One of the speakers in support of the motion had collected an impressive array of facts and figures from other African countries to prove his point; and he certainly succeeded in making it appear that more importance was attached to age in our town than was the case elsewhere on the continent. The member of staff who was chairman for the occasion carefully kept the debate from going off course, and speakers were prevented from discussing whether any progress toward the magic goal of self-government was possible under the rule of old men; but certainly it was in precisely this direction that I found my thoughts turning again and again. Until that afternoon I had found myself too absorbed in my studies to give more than a passing thought to politics, municipal or national. But in that somewhat flippant debate I thought I caught a fleeting glimpse of two great truths which have remained with me since. The first was that a constitution on paper can be a very different thing from a constitution in practice, because social attitudes are far more important than ordinances and laws in determining the effective shape of a government. The second truth I glimpsed was that the older a man gets the less disposed he is to change the political system to which he is accustomed; and that therefore if national development requires radical political change, as is the case in subject territories, sooner or later the centre of political influence must be made to shift from the older generation to the younger.

Having thought thus far, I cannot remember pursuing the

matter any further at the time, either in word, deed or thought. I had glimpsed what might have been a mere mirage, and was soon plodding again devotedly across the arid wastes of the School Certificate syllabus, toward a more immediate and more tangible goal. But even mirages leave their mark on the mind; and some of the speeches made at that debate were to return to me with crystal clarity during my student days, when we were analysing with the usual student intentness the causes of our real or imagined polit-ical ills.

Two weeks before the fateful examination began, I was indiscreet enough to fight the principal's son. He was a fellow fifth-former with whom, up till then, I had had no quarrel at all. He was inclined to be a little overbearing at times; but then a flint needs contact with another flint in order to spark, and I had been forced to develop from the start an easygoing and tolerant disposition. I suppose as the examina-tion drew nearer our nerves became tauter and our tempers shorter. When during a discussion in our classroom about careers Samuel declared unnecessarily loudly that he be-lieved all persons who came from the North should return to it to find employment, I suddenly felt my anger rising like a column of mercury. I asked him why, in as calm a voice as I could assume; he replied with a sneer by quoting a Sagresan proverb whose meaning was roughly that even a man who does not know where he is going to ought at least to know where he has come from; and the general laughter which greeted it brought my temper to boiling point. I was tall and well built, but so was he: three strides took me to his side, and one blow floored him. By the time the senior prefect succeeded in separating us, Sagresan blood and Lokko blood had mingled on the floor. Moreover, as is the custom with us, the fight was as much verbal as physical, and a torrent of abuse directed mainly against the other's ante-cedents was flowing out of each battered mouth.

31

We were bloody, sweaty, and dusty when it was over, but still only partly through our respective stocks of abuse. Nothing more than a heightened respect each for the other might have come out of the fight, had Samuel been a boarder. Unfortunately for both of us, however, he lived very much under his august father's eye, and the marks I had succeeded in leaving on his face were too distinctive to be hidden by any sort of artifice. I prepared for the worst (prepared in spirit, that is, for physical preparations were known to be unavailing at such times). The summons to the principal's office duly came after lunch the same day.

He was quite impartial, I'll say that for him. We were both arched over his desk and inscribed across our rumps with two dozen strokes of a bamboo four-footer. Then we were made to shake hands with each other and sent off for a walk together along the beach and back (this was the principal's usual way of dealing with a pair of fighters, and one which usually made bosom friends of them). That thrashing, and the walk which followed, gave me the moments of deepest mortification I have experienced, and drove home to me the utter futility and wastefulness of making issues of tribal divisions, in a land where so much else required our attentions and our energies. Having heard from us how the fight started, the principal might so easily have wasted our time and his reading us a long patriotic sermon on the essential brotherhood of all the people of Songhai. Such a theme would have made him appear to me a hypocrite and to Samuel a traitor – for we both knew only too well that the differences between us were real, if not deep. Instead, we were made to share a fellowship of misery and humiliation which linked us together more effectively than any half-believed fiction about cultural or ethnic affinities could have succeeded in doing.

So we walked in silence along that beach under a burnished sky, lost in thoughts which we were later to discover were very similar. We were only half-conscious of the presence behind us of one of the school prefects who had been detailed by the principal to dog our footsteps (and report any failure to complete our penance). After this we avoided each other for a whole week, not out of spite but out of embarrassment. It was only after this feeling had worn off, and the curious questionings and malicious sallies which the incident had inspired in our classmates had begun to wear thin, that Samuel and I saw in each other's eyes across the chapel aisle one evening a message in response to which we met afterwards in an empty classroom. What passed between us then was more, much more, than mere reconciliation; more even than the making and sealing of what was to became a lifelong friendship – though certainly both these were achieved. Far more important was the joint pledging of ourselves to an ideal – the ideal of helping to create in our time a country which would achieve both strength and freedom through unity, and the subordination to that ideal of all tribal loyalties. That we both remained entirely faithful to that ideal will, I believe, be seen from the rest of my story.

So the examination came and passed; and the results which were published after a seemingly interminable period of waiting showed that the long hours of study had not been in vain. 'Grandpa', Samuel and I were amongst the proud holders of first-grade certificates, and this meant that the way was open for us to win scholarships for university studies. I had hardly thought about this possibility, mainly because I was doubtful as to whether my English had yet reached a sufficiently high standard. The evening the results came out, Samuel and I walked together up to the top of College Hill to reflect on next steps. A silver filigree of stars was above our heads, a golden filigree of lights at our feet. The moon was rising and full, and had thrown a glittering silver coin into the fountain by which we sat. We sang, sang at the top of our powerful young lungs, in sheer relief and exhilaration.

Cars, buses and pedestrians passed us on their way to and from the university college which was housed in brand-new buildings on the slopes of the hill. A passing group of students offered to fetch us the college doctor. But we could afford to laugh back with them and to continue our song.

Near the upper limit of the college site, there was a small amphitheatre. Samuel and I took the stage and acted to an invisible audience as much of *Macbeth* (one of our set-books) as we could remember. This was not, I think, to get it out of our systems, for we both had developed a genuine affection for Shakespeare. We wished finally to prove to ourselves that the examiners' assessment of our intelligence and knowledge had been entirely accurate. We were at the zenith of self-conceit.

When we re-emerged somewhat hoarse and dusty, it was late. A nearby college staff bungalow glowed with cosy light, and the sounds of B.B.C. community hymn-singing reached us from its open windows, to be strangely echoed by the rediffusion loud-speakers in humbler households in the town below. The moon was now high in the sky, silvering the very air we breathed. To our right, and forming a bizarre accompaniment to the hymns, the sound of drumming rose throbbing from a nearby village. Both of us realised the symbolism of our position in place and time; buffeted by confused crosscurrents of native and alien cultures, standing excitedly on the fringes of academic life. We stood there for a moment, silent and thoughtful. Then we turned and made our way back to town in a mood no less elated, though much less boisterously so.

CHAPTER FOUR

FOUR MONTHS LATER Samuel and I sailed to England.
Reassured as to my linguistic ability, I wished to read
honours English; whilst Samuel was bound for medical
school. The local university college could offer us satisfactory
courses in neither field, and so the Songhai Government,
which was not in a position to deny either the usefulness of
these courses or our own capacity to benefit from them, gave
us full scholarships to pursue them. The only conditions laid
down were that we should return, on the successful comple-
tion of the course, to serve our country for five years (a stipu-
lation which we both regarded then as unnecessary), and that
we should not marry without Government's permission until
we had qualified. This latter condition we found positively
mystifying, but likely to prove even less onerous, we were
sure, than the first. We signed the bond with an elaborate
flourish. Then for four months we received a large volume of
advice (mainly contradictory) and winter clothing (mainly
unwearable) from friends and relatives who had already
made the pilgrimage. England was universally regarded on
the West Coast then in the light of a finishing school which
left its mark on the traveller's poise, speech, clothes-sense,
and matrimonial prospects; not to speak of his educational
attainments, and value on the employment market.

So the day came when we left the little group of friends
and relatives on the wharf and slithered down the slippery
steps to the pitching launch which was to convey us to the
liner riding at anchor in the harbour. I had spent the last
fortnight before sailing with my family in Lokko, and one
of my brothers had come down to Sagresa to see me off (my

father and mother preferring to bid me farewell in their own home). As I squeezed my brother's hand for the last time, he left in mine a large, uncut diamond. He told me that it was my father's wish that I should keep this always with me in my journey away from home, to remind me that the whole treasure of my people's faith and affection went with me. The possession without a licence of uncut diamonds was at that time illegal in Songhai, and the great risk my father and brother had run added value and meaning to the token. I smothered it in my handkerchief with a feeling of deep emotion. Now, as I write, part of that same stone, still uncut and undistinguished in appearance, is before me, the material possession I hold most dear. In it I see hidden the glorious flame of Africa's spirit, the richness of her wealth, and the sharp edge of her energy. It has become for me the penetrating star of African freedom, a light by which to rouse a sleeping giant.

But these were later thoughts. For now the rain streamed down in a curtain of endless, slanting grey between the tossing launch to whose rail I clung and the little group waving farewell at the top of the wharf steps. The mooring ropes were cast off and the gap widened quickly, until the outlines of glistening umbrellas and raincoats blurred and dissolved. As we passed close to a waterside backyard, a young girl of about my age was taking advantage of the rainfall, as I had so often done, to take a bath out of doors with no more elaborate equipment than a piece of soap. Her face radiant with the vast enjoyment she was deriving from her simple toilet, she threw her head back, shut her eyes and laughed out her happiness as she worked the soap up into thick lather all over her skin. The string of red beads round her waist disappeared momentarily beneath the lather, to re-emerge a moment later as a shower of rain water swept the lather down her legs in a rush. On a sudden impulse I waved to her, and so received my final farewell from my homeland. She waved back vigorously, still laughing, her white teeth flashing, and an instant later was lost to my sight.

Africans are very conscious of the importance of symbolism in life; and that happy, bathing girl has always summed up for me all that has been worth returning to Africa for. My last farewell was also, for me, my most meaningful. I have never, so far as I know, set eyes on this particular girl again; but neither have I ever forgotten the intensity of her happiness or the utter purity and innocence of its source. I did not need to be a hedonist to perceive that she had obtained the highest good man can hope for on earth, and had done so without sacrificing anything of any consequence to herself or anyone else. To be completely happy, and yet not to have to pay too much for it in any way, physical or spiritual – this is perhaps what we all live for ultimately. And yet the capacity to do this would become increasingly lost to the peoples of Africa, as I could have told even then from my own limited experience. But to have glimpsed the ideal was enough to impress indelibly on my mind that all would in the end be lost if, in gaining the world, we were to lose our souls.

The hull of the ship loomed above me, black and glistening; the inside, white and hospital-smelling, sickened me. But this sensation was not to last long, and within a few hours of sailing both Samuel and I had found our sea legs and were enjoying the voyage. As Government scholars (the only two such on board from Songhai), we were travelling first-class. Two hopes had been aroused in us by the knowledge of this arrangement: that we should have the opportunity of mixing with Englishmen and talking to them (our thirst for knowledge was now newly whetted); and that we should be able to eat our fill of really good food (for we were, after all, little more than schoolboys still).

Our first meal killed both hopes. The food we found to be execrable, although five years of school food might have been expected to make us both thoroughly tolerant. An ideal

37

meal, in our view, consisted of one course, containing something solid and bulky, well smothered in oil, well spiced and peppered, and topped with enough pieces of meat and fish to make the leftovers edible. Instead we were offered a dozen courses, each inconseqential, fiddling and tasteless – a slice of fish and a crescent of lemon; three spoonfuls of soup whose only interest lay in its French name; a triangular slice of toasted bread coated with egg, and so on. The fear that this might be a foretaste of our diet for the next few years was only partially relieved by the knowledge that we had well-filled boxes of foodstuff with us in the ship's hold.

Our hope of learning more about the British, their language, customs, history, and social conventions, at first hand from our fellow-passengers was even more bitterly disappointed. We had looked forward so much to escaping from the strained atmosphere which then made real contact between white and black on the West Coast impossible. It is true, as I have said, that we were only just out of school; but we were no younger perhaps than some of the more junior British colonial officers who shared that dining room with us. I believe many of them would have been as glad as we should have been to be able to let the barriers down and draw us into their circle. But it would have meant a flouting of the code of social behaviour in which they had been drilled, and this was altogether beyond them to do. It would, for example, have involved defying the unwritten laws laid down by the shipping line to prevent Europeans and Africans from coming into too close or too frequent contact on board. The gradual realisation that such a policy existed was the first bitter blow to the hopeful optimism with which we had set out from our native land. We watched the chief steward taking infinite pains with the seating arrangements at that first meal, to prevent white and black from sitting at the same table. We noticed the deck steward's raised eyebrows a little later when we dived into the swimming pool – which happened to be otherwise empty at the time. It was as if the ship's crew had been instructed to make us feel that we were in first-class on sufferance only, and not by right; and might be kicked back into steerage, where we belonged, at any time. To break away from this attitude (which was, incidentally, more marked in the ship's stewards than in its officers), and to break the habits formed on the West Coast of somewhat patronising behaviour toward the African, was something we perhaps had no right to expect of any white man on that ship. But we did expect it; and our sense of ostracism and humiliation mounted so rapidly that on the second day out we avoided all the public rooms except the dining saloon, and magnified our grievances by examining them from every possible angle in the security of our cabin. We found three fellow-students from other West African colonies whose experiences were very similar to ours, and our resentment against our white fellow passengers was soon assuming quite unjustified proportions.

It is perhaps a pity that the British, with their traditional reserve, were the most successful of African imperial powers. For reserve shown toward a once-subject people is at once interpreted as prejudice. Two pairs of eyes meet across a ship's lounge or smoking room: a copy of *The Times* is promptly interposed across the line of vision by the Briton, and the African sucks his teeth and curses him in his heart. In fact, of course, the Briton would have made exactly the same gesture if his eyes had met almost any other strange ones. And so gestures create attitudes, and attitudes in turn give colour to gestures, and the waters are soon poisoned almost beyond cleansing.

But, in our case, not quite. We were young, full of new plans, ambitions, enthusiasms. And we knew at heart we could not possibly be happier in the company of foreigners than we were amongst our own people; so we still succeeded in enjoying the voyage, with all its novelty for us and its

39

sense of adventure. At Las Palmas, the last port of call before Liverpool, the five of us were the first of the passengers to go ashore sight-seeing, and the last to return to the ship. We laughed together at the promptness with which the Spanish taxi-driver in whose ancient vehicle we found ourselves produced photographs of seductive senoritas from his breast pocket. We laughed even louder at his utter discomfiture on discovering that five healthy young men could have no desire at all to visit his principals. Instead we entered the quaint old shops and markets where everyone unashamedly sought to relieve you of as many pesetas – or, better still, shillings – as they could; and the massive cathedral. Here we were dismayed to see that the same mercenary tradition was maintained. The robed choirboy guides charged you to go in, charged you again to mount the tower in a lift into which they had almost pushed you, tried to sell you literature you did not want and could not read, and made you wonder whether they would not charge you to leave the building. We were depressed by the contrast between the wealth of the vestments and holy plate in the cathedral, and the ragged if cheerful poverty of the street urchins teeming round us in the streets outside.

I have always found great extremes of wealth disturbing. As I moved from Lokko to Sagresa, and then to Europe, I found the social gaps widening at each stage. Associating these gaps, therefore, with the 'Western' way of life, I felt uneasy and dissatisfied; and it was with relief that I learned later that the association was not quite as inevitable as I had at first imagined.

On our last night on board before arriving at Liverpool, five very excited young men gathered in one of the cabins, whilst most of the passengers were dancing away the evening in a farewell party on deck. We were excited at the prospect of our first sight of Britain, the country from which had originated so much we admired and so much we resented in the West African scene. At first we discussed only our immediate future, where we were going to study, what courses we were going to take, how we were going to earn the extra pocket money we anticipated we should all need during the long vacation, and so on. But presently the conversation turned to the more remote future.

'Are any of you planning to go into politics when you return home?' – It was Ademola, short, slight, very dark, asking. He had handsome tribal markings on his cheeks.

'As far as I am concerned, it is one thing at a time,' I replied at once, and there was a general murmur of assent. 'I am not going to begin to think about politics, or even whether or not I ought to enter into it, until I have qualified.'

'But some of our leaders are ruining our country even now,' persisted Ademola. 'Look at the way they want to split my country up. It's a downright crime, and they all deserve good long prison sentences for it.' Ademola was going to study law, and was very fond of passing sentence on people of whom he disapproved.

'I agree,' said Okoli, a light-skinned, spectacled engineering student. 'And I think too that we young men must begin at least talking and reading about the political situation back at home now, whilst we are students with fresh ideas and no commitments or political bonds of any kind. I feel sure that if all the African students in the United Kingdom now could come together as *students* to think and act together, we could all have self-government in ten years.'

Appiah, a tall, broad-shouldered, handsome man rose up on one elbow on one of the bunks and spat forcefully out of the porthole. 'There's only one way to deal with the white man,' he said, with a smile strangely in contrast with his words and his tone. 'You have got to produce *deeds* to convince him that you can beat him and defeat him whichever way he turns. He does not really listen to big words. It is a crowd of ten thousand outside Government House that does

41

the trick, or a journey by a few leaders to prison in the cause others only *talk* about. That is what is needed, and all the territories in Africa must realise this quickly.'

'We all seem to have different techniques, from what I read.' Samuel munched thoughtfully at an apple brought up from the dining saloon. 'We are going slowly in Songhai, because we seem to be plagued with old men in charge of everything. ('Hear, hear,' I interposed hurriedly.) But I don't think you will ever get the people of Sagresa, even the young ones, to strike or revolt against the Government. We pride ourselves, all of us, on being ancient and loyal.'

'Emphasis on "ancient",' snorted Appiah contemptuously. 'Every British imperialist must chortle up his sleeve when he hears you people using that phrase. Why don't you give it up? It hurts me every time I hear it!'

'Here, hold on, hold on, hold on!' Mensah, the fifth member of our group, emerged from the bathroom where he had been drying himself after a shower, and listening to us through the half-open connecting door. As the weather had turned colder on the northward journey, our hot showers had become more and more frequent, and taken not so much either for hygiene or the novelty of it (as they had been at first) but for their thermal value. Mensah was dressed in the full glory of a set of new, full-length woollen underwear which he told us he had ordered out specially from Lennards for use on this passage, and which we all secretly envied him. However, he looked so distinctly odd in this, his first appearance in the unusual garb, with only his feet, hands and head emerging blackly from the tickly looking white material, that we all burst into gales of laughter. An angry hammering promptly thundered from the bulkhead. Someone in the next cabin had evidently stayed away from the party not to laugh and talk but to sleep.

'If that garment had been brown, Darwin's theories would have needed no further proof,' said Appiah; and more shouts of laughter and more angry blows followed.

'Look, we'd better be quieter; it's after midnight, and we don't want these people to get an even worse impression of Africans than some of them already seem to have.' Samuel's quiet words brought us to our senses, and we all lowered our voices. We were all to learn later that our native lack of restraint could become the source of much misunderstanding, for example, between British landladies and African students. It took us a long time to admit that most of the fault in such circumstances lay with us who, as guests in another man's country, bore the responsibility of modifying our behaviour to avoid giving offence to our hosts.

'As I was saying before being rudely interrupted,' said Mensah, drawing a pair of bright blue silk pyjamas over the garments which were the cause of so much mirth. 'Hold on! Don't forget about the tortoise and the hare. Some African colonies seem to live on the edge of danger the whole time, simply because they are moving so fast – like a lorry driver racing along a dirt road at sixty miles an hour. If the tyre does burst, he will have a much more serious accident than the man who is proceeding at a cautious thirty miles an hour. We must not condemn the tactics of the slower territories until we see which of us achieves the most stable self-government.'

Appiah began to wax philosophical. 'You know what, I believe sooner or later all our countries will win self-government. It's bound to happen. After all, we Africans are a superior race, you know! Look at our physical characteristics! Aren't our curly hair, thick lips, and erect carriage proof that our stage of evolution is more advanced than that reached by the whites? After all, apes have straight hair and thin lips, and walk slightly crouched. Moreover if the aim of civilisation is the achievement of social harmony, who is more civilised, the African or the European? Look at the suicide, insanity and divorce figures!'

'*Apartheid* in reverse. And absolute nonsense of course!' Mensah climbed into his bunk in disgust, and turned his face to the bulkhead. 'Go and tell them that at Hyde Park Corner. I dare you! At least it will prove what I've always suspected – that you bushmen from up-country have more nerve than brains.'

What was very evident, however, about our attitudes that evening was that although we had a lively interest in *political* progress in our territories, we evinced a blissful unconcern about any other forms of progress, social, educational, or economic. We believed the political key would open all the other doors. But we were determined for the present to concentrate on our studies and leave active politics to others.

After some further talk, during the course of which we agreed to keep in touch with each other, we dispersed to our cabins. Samuel and I completed the final items of packing, and took a last look out of our porthole at the lights of the English coastline and of passing ships winking their welcome to us. Then we turned in, schoolboys once more in the sleeplessness of our bright-eyed excitement.

CHAPTER FIVE

L I V E R P O O L next day was grey, cold, wet and foggy; and the promised land looked most unpromising from the deck of the ship. Once ashore, however, the towering buildings, massed traffic, and attractive shops kept us staring and gaping whilst waiting for our trains to various parts of the country. The sight of white people *en masse* was itself something which required some getting used to; but the thing that took us really aback was our first sight of a white man sweeping a gutter. He was a short, seedy-looking, rather dirty man, with heavy working boots and stained, well-worn clothes, but unmistakably a white man nevertheless; and actually standing right down in the gutter sweeping it, collecting the rubbish on a shovel and tipping it into a wheelbarrow. We stood in utter disbelief, at some little distance from him, expecting him at any moment either to vanish like a gremlin down the nearest drain, or else to turn dark brown. I suppose if you had asked us beforehand who swept gutters in England, we should have replied, after a moment or two's reflection, that we supposed some of the English drains, at least, must have the honour of being swept by white men; for even all the stowaways and workless migrants from Africa and the West Indies could not provide enough labour for so many menial tasks. But no one had prepared us beforehand by any such question; and the sight of that man almost felled us.

'Thank God for bringing me here,' breathed Appiah reverently, the first amongst us to recover his breath. 'I always suspected there was some good reason for my coming to Britain.'

And I think that summed up how most of us felt. We did not lose respect for the white man – very far from it. What we did lose however (and long overdue was the loss), was an illusion created by the rôle the white man plays in Africa: that he is a kind of demigod whose hands must never get dirty, who must not be allowed to carry anything heavier than a portfolio or wield any implement heavier than a pen. Without realising it, we had come to think of the white man only in the rôle of missionary, civil servant, or senior business executive, one who was always behind the desk, never in front of it. We saw him as one who always gave orders, never took them, who could have any job he liked for the asking. So to realise that that man was perfectly happy working in that gutter (snatches of his melancholy whistling reached us faintly where we stood) was a most salutary experience. It was now possible for us to like the white man. For before you can like (as distinct from merely admiring or emulating), you must feel kinship, a shared humanity, the possibility of common experiences and destinies. As we resumed our walk past the sweeper, he looked up and grinned cheerfully at us, leaning for a moment on his brush. We waved and grinned back; and in that mute exchange of greetings there was erased in a moment the memory of the behaviour of the stewards on board. The latter had acted as if the gods had decreed that the black man should minister and the white man be ministered unto, and that they were stewards and we passengers only by special dispensation. Our friend the road-sweeper, on the other hand, was so far from harbouring any such notions that he had found time to give us, in his own way, a welcome to Liverpool.

We were soon to find, as countless thousands of colonial students in the United Kingdom must have found, that the Britisher at home is an altogether different creature, and a much more lovable one, than the Britisher overseas. Perhaps, though, the same applies to most people. Abroad, we are in a minority, and a minority always feels and acts insecure. Abroad, too, we all to a greater or lesser extent are conscious of treading a stage; of having to live up to, or to live down, a national reputation. The white man abroad has to prove that he is superior to the black man; the black man abroad has to prove that he is not inferior to the white man. The proving of both cases involves much play-acting, much assumption of false rôles. The only solution is for the colonial student to be offered, and to accept unreservedly, a 'home from home' on the hearth of a British family; a family not necessarily wealthier than that of our road-sweeper, but certainly no less free from false ideas as to the proper position of white men and black men vis-à-vis each other. For when members of the two races can be brought to share a home in the fullest sense of the words, to feel genuinely 'at home', façades fall, pretence ceases, masks are removed, and it is rare indeed that the real man does not attract. My years in the United Kingdom were to teach me that the ordinary British home can undo the harm done by die-hard imperialists far more effectively than all the money invested in Colonial Development and Welfare Funds and Colonial Students' Hostels (indispensable as these are), and all the Colonial Office receptions, dances, tours, and conferences put together.

However, as my train to Newcastle raced through the Lancashire countryside on that wet September morning, my thoughts were on more humdrum things than finding solutions to the problem of race relations in Britain. I was alone now, my friends having dispersed in various directions. It had been particularly hard to say good-bye to Samuel, who was bound for Birmingham. My fellow-passengers in the compartment were behaving as though they had not seen me, and I supposed that this must be the traditional way of welcoming a stranger in Britain. I wondered about my luggage – would it be all right in the guard's van? Were any

47

boxes or bottles broken, was any palm oil spilt? I wondered about the hostel I was to stay in until I could find permanent lodgings – would I find any other Africans there? Would I be able to eat the food, stand up to the weather? Suddenly I felt terribly lonely in that compartment. I suppose it is not an unusual experience to be attacked by a sense of extreme solitude when one is amongst a lot of people, if for any reason one is cut off from intercourse with those people. Here was I being transported from busy station to busy station, through towns and cities teeming with more people than I had ever seen together before in my life, with a constantly changing group of people with me in the compartment; and yet I had a feeling that I was all alone for the first time in my experience. I shut my eyes in my corner and tried to allow the rhythm of the wheels to lull me to sleep; but I was in the grip of a sense of anticlimax, and my closed eyes were invaded by tears, not sleep. It was a feeling similar to the one I had experienced during my second night in Sagresa, though less acute and shorter-lived. For this time I had far too much of importance to think about and, as the train drew into Newcastle Central Station, to do.

About half an hour before it did so, however, I was to draw fresh courage and inspiration from an unexpected source. I was gazing out of the window at a landscape frequently dominated by the gaunt, blackened superstructures of pit-heads, when, as the train swung round a curve and over a viaduct, my breath was completely taken away for an instant by the sight of Durham Cathedral. We may have passed other cathedrals on that journey as massive and as strikingly situated – I cannot tell. Certainly I noticed none to compare with this. It seemed to float proudly above the smoky rooftops, gradually turning on its own axis as we described an arc around it, in order, so it seemed, to show itself off to the best advantage. The massive towers, the age-mellowed stone whose colour blended so naturally with that of the foliage around it on the banks of the River Wear; above all the mute drama of human faith and achievement played on a stage set by God in the elbow of a river and watched over by the vigilance of eight centuries: all this somehow gave me a starting point for my new studies, and so helped me to forget my temporary sense of loneliness. I was going to study English – not only a language, but a whole culture. Here was a massive physical creation of a people who, while not originating in these islands, had contributed so much to shaping the character of their people. I felt for the first time then the powerful aesthetic appeal of the heritage of Britain which was to be the subject of my study. My main motives, up to this point, had been bread-and-butter ones – to master a language and become acquainted with a culture which, for better or for worse, were of great social and commercial importance in my country. Durham made me realise that, like the work of those Norman builders, my labours must be inspired by considerations other than the purely material, if they were to produce results whose success would have some degree of permanence. I determined to return to Durham at the earliest opportunity, and to go elsewhere in Britain, as occasion offered, where in 'a thing of beauty' I might find 'a joy for ever'.

I was soon very comfortably settled in at the Colonial Students' Club in Newcastle. It was situated in Leazes Terrace, opposite a small park, within walking distance of the vast Town Moor, and a short trolley-bus ride from a lovely glen, Jesmond Dene. To make my satisfaction complete, King's College, the Newcastle division of the University of Durham, of which I was now a proud undergraduate, had its main buildings, including its library, only a few hundred yards away, and I was able to plunge straight into my reading. It is difficult for me to describe the pleasure with which I gazed at the row upon row of bookshelves in the library. The opportunity to read as much as one cared on

49

any subject which caught one's interest was something, I knew well enough, which not one in ten thousand of my countrymen was given. I felt I could endure any difficulties of food, weather and loneliness whilst this opportunity remained mine.

In fact, I never really felt lonely again after those first few hours in the train from Liverpool. Not only were there many other Africans at King's, but I found in these north-country folk a warm friendliness, and in most of my British fellow-students a constant readiness to offer companionship and advice. How adaptable is the human animal in circumstances such as these! Within a few weeks, I was moving alone through the streets of Newcastle and mixing with the students in their work and play with a freedom and an ease I never dreamed beforehand would have come to me. Even the physical adaptation to diet and climate was soon effected, and all my earlier uncertainties and anxieties were forgotten. I wrote happy letters home assuring my mother and father that they had nothing to worry about at all, and that everything had worked out to good advantage.

Some of the ways of the British students did appear to me distinctly odd, as no doubt mine did to them. I found, for example, their refusal to admit the necessity for a daily bath, even in high summer, a little disconcerting. I had been brought up to believe that cleanliness is next to godliness and also lies next to the skin. Whenever I would hear students in Britain referring to that curious institution of theirs, the 'bath-night', as though it were a special and not very welcome weekly recurrence, I would think of the little stream which splashed under the bridge in Lokko. It was a temperamental stream: during the dry season it would shrink to a mere trickle, and at the height of the rains it would swell to a boiling, pounding cataract which could sweep grown men away. But every day, rainy season or dry, it would be the scene of busy laundry and toilet activity for a large number of people. What better and more sensible time to wash your clothes than when you yourself are having your bath? The water was soft and cool, and the rocks, hard and smooth, were perfect for beating clothes against. There was only one unwritten law about this admirable practice – no mixed bathing; and a good beating and cursing for any Peeping Tom. And throughout history conquered peoples have taught their conquerors good habits. The British in Africa also bathe assiduously whatever the weather.

I found that in contrast to the casual attitude of many British students toward personal cleanliness, the concern of the British generally over the tidiness of their homes, streets, gardens and parks was limitless. Here I believed they could teach us much. Everywhere you went, you sensed a tradition of providing a place for everything and making sure that place was used as intended. Surface water, sewage, waste paper, old rags, bottles and bones, even smoke; everything must be properly disposed of. The proper conservation and controlled use of all national resources, if necessary in a relatively wealthy country such as this, I thought, must be a thousand times more so for us.

I could not help noticing, too, the individualism of the Britisher, and the looseness of his family ties and obligations, as compared with ours. We were brought up to have an intense pride in our family, and an intense loyalty to it; and to feel that that pride and loyalty must extend to the most distant relative known to us. The word 'family' means more to an African than it does to a European; and many of us smile quietly when we hear British people talking about family life in their country. How little of it there really is! I remember how no one either in Lokko or in Sagresa, old or young, took any important decision without first discussing the pros and cons with every available relative. A wedding, christening, funeral or initiation ceremony not attended by every member of the family who was not overseas would be unthinkable. In times of adversity, there were literally scores and scores of relatives to console one; in times of prosperity a similar number turned up to share both your joy and your material wealth. A man who merely disliked you cursed you; a man who hated you cursed your family. It was all really an elaborate and most effective system of social security; and through it the very great extremes of wealth and poverty which have brought suffering and injustice into the social life of so many European countries (and revolution and bloodshed to some) have thus far been avoided in Africa. We had a joke amongst ourselves in the hostel in Newcastle that the Englishman treats his dog as he should his nephew, and his nephew as merely another man's son.

This first year passed very quickly for me. I often went back to Durham to drink my fill of its beauty; and I loved to stand on Palace Green, with castle on one side and cathedral on the other, trying to picture the proud Normans at work on those magnificent structures. I also often travelled north to Berwick-on-Tweed, marvelling there at the perfectly devised contrasts of its bridges. From there I would travel westwards through the lovely Border country with its rolling, stream-laced terrain, its old, thick-walled homesteads and castles, and its untutored rustics whose English was so deeply accented that, strain as I might, I could not follow a word they uttered. South again to Hadrian's wall, again to let my imagination roam; to try to picture in my mind's eye the life of those distant centuries in which the language and culture I was engaged in studying were gradually evolving, assimilating as they did so many varied strains from other lands. Most of these journeys I undertook alone; for I had become disposed to introspection and to thinking and studying alone. I think I had as many friends as any other student in Newcastle, and could enjoy a party or a dance well enough. But when it came to my studies (and I regarded these visits to places of natural beauty or historical interest as a vital part of my studies), I found I could absorb the atmosphere of the place much more effectively alone, without distraction.

So it was I set out at the beginning of my first long vacation on that fateful visit to the Lake District. I had joined the Youth Hostel Association; and, in order to make my not over-generous allowance stretch out as far as possible, decided to hitch-hike to the Lakes and around them, and to stay in the Youth Hostels all the way. I had become a great believer in the Youth Hostel idea; for in it I could see the opportunity both of obtaining a close acquaintance of the English countryside at little cost, and of getting to know a large number of people of widely differing interests and occupations. This latter consideration I regarded as important, not because I liked meeting people (for I did not particularly), but because it was, I knew, a most effective way of enlarging my English vocabulary. I chose the Lake District because of its associations with so many of the authors I was studying; and I stuffed into my rucksack as many of the well-loved English classics as I conveniently could.

The journey from Newcastle to Keswick I reckoned to do easily in a day. I found that the lorry drivers were for the most part only too ready to stop and pick me up, though many private cars slowed down and then thought better of it on seeing the unexpected complexion of the hitch-hiker. No doubt I presented a rather strange sight in my corduroy trousers and khaki shirt, and with my bulging rucksack on a harness on my back. I can readily understand the battle between curiosity and self-preservation which the sight must have touched off in many a motorist, and can forgive the victory of self-preservation. Besides, the Second World War was then on.

My longest leg in one vehicle was thumbed from just outside Hexham to Carlisle, in a big timber truck. The driver was alone in his cab, and at his invitation I climbed up into the seat beside him. I found him a genial, plump, red-faced fellow who, I immediately decided, must be precisely the type of fellow Dickens had in mind when he conceived the character of Mr Pickwick. My friend was more than a little amused at finding an African in this unusual garb. For some time he drove slowly and examined me carefully.

'Well, well, well,' he managed to say at length. 'Who would 'a thought of this on a fine mornin'? And where are you headin' for, young man?'

'Keswick, to tour the Lake District.'

'You're a mighty long way from home, ain't you? And where might your home be?'

'Sagresa.'

'And where's that?'

I smiled tolerantly. 'It's the capital of Songhai.'

'Oh! That there Portuguese place! And here am I just itching to tell you how I feel the British Empire's a damn hypocritical set-up.'

'Songhai *is* British.'

'Well, is it now!' His jovial face creased up with smiles and he chortled deep down in his throat. 'Why don't they ever tell me these things?'

'Those who should tell you don't usually know themselves,' I ventured. He turned and gave me a long hard look; but I think it was the naturalness of my English rather than the content of my words that had surprised him. 'I am a student at King's College, so I know just how little even my fellow-students really know about their Empire.'

My new-found friend had quite recovered his good humour now. 'There's a hell of a lot of it, you know,' he said, 'from what I remember of me long-lost school-days. So you're bound for Keswick, eh? Very sensible too. You'll have a grand time amongst them Lakes, I can promise you that. But is this how you travel around . . . er . . . Songo, did you say, hitch-hiking and that, I mean?'

'No; but we have plenty of lorries – mammy-lorries we call them, as they are usually full of women going to market. They have some very amusing inscriptions painted on them too.'

'Let's hear some of 'em. You never know, perhaps the week before I'm due to retire I might have some fun brightening up this old bus just to see what 'ud happen!' And again the deep chuckle as he changed his gears down with a graceful, easy, well-practised movement.

'"No Sweat, No Sweet." And rather ominous but well-meant sentiments such as "In God We Trust", "God is my refuge", "One More River to Cross", and so on.' His resonant laugh punctuated my words.

'You get many accidents?'

'Yes, a lot, considering the fact that our traffic is not as dense as yours. But the drivers usually take good care to escape unhurt; and, if they can make it, to disappear before anyone asks them any questions.'

'How's that? No police?'

'Not many up-country.'

He emitted a sound which was a mixture of grunt and sigh, and which might have denoted anything from envy to incredulity. In the distance a roadside café came into view, with a cluster of heavy lorries on the open ground around it.

'You'll come in and have a bite and a cup o' tea with me chums and me, won't you, young 'un?' he asked. And then, as we came a little closer, 'Oh, I see old Charlie is there – that's his truck on the far side, the big red eight-wheeler. Now he's a rare old bird, not much eddication perhaps if you compare him with you and your friends at college; but plenty of good common sense, lots o' little bits of odd know-ledge and news picked up from all over the world – he's travelled a bit in his time, has old Charlie, and can tell and take a joke with the best of them.' Our gears grated slightly,

55

the brakes hissed, and we turned in and parked neatly amongst the other trucks.

I felt at first a little chary about accepting my friend's invitation. One could not be sure that all lorry drivers would be as ready as he had been to welcome the intrusion into their company of an African who was, in addition, what they would have called 'one of the eddicated'. But I was genuinely thirsty, and could not resist the thought of having, not so much a 'cup o' tea' (I had not yet acquired that particular English habit) but a lemonade or fruit drink of some kind.

We entered a small, low-ceilinged room filled with small tables on which were plates, cups and saucers, and cutlery, but no cloths. There were a dozen or so men seated in small groups at the tables, and most of them seemed to have a greeting for my driver as we entered. He chose a table where there were two empty seats, and I could sense the curious looks turned in my direction from all parts of the room as we sat down.

'Friend of mine hitch-hiking to the Lakes,' said Joe (as I at once discovered he was called) by way of explanation and perhaps apology to the others at the table. 'What's your name, lad? And don't be afraid of them, you know. They won't bite you. They're all very nice boys.'

'Kamara,' I said, feeling more than a little uncomfortable at the amount of attention I was receiving. It was the first time I had found myself amongst a group of Britishers most of whom were meeting a man of my race for the first time. There was a brief, awkward pause. Then a big broad-shouldered man with a bronzed, weather-beaten face and watery eyes sitting opposite me broke the ice. He leaned across the table, gripped my hand and shook it with a cordiality better befitting the reunion of long-lost friends. 'You're right welcome amongst us,' he said. 'No better place than the Lakes for a holiday, no better way of travelling than hitch-hiking, and no better company to meet on the way than the present company assembled – although I say so meself.'

'Good old Charlie,' said Joe. 'Nothing ever robs you of words for long.' "So this is Charlie the traveller," I thought to myself, looking at him with fresh interest, and feeling an instinctive liking for him already. Indeed, in a very few minutes, my feeeling of strangeness had worn off, as those at the other tables appeared to forget about me, and those at ours drew me into their conversation with a naturalness which I should never have believed possible. They were a forthright, unsophisticated crowd, with a wonderful fund of tales at the tips of their tongues; some witty, some sad, some lugubrious, many smutty, others merely tall, but all, even the corniest, fascinating to me. This was just what I wanted – an opportunity to listen to good round twentieth-century English as used by those whose formal education had been limited, but whose experience of life and whose contact with other people living in those islands had been of the very widest. Charlie had, indeed, as Joe had told me, travelled widely outside Britain, and he soon revealed to me that he had spent several days being 'pressure cooked', as he chose to put it, in a troopship at anchor in Sagresa harbour during the war. But he declared himself prepared to forgive and forget that experience (it was not quite clear whether it was I or the War Office who was to be favoured with his gracious pardon). He then went on to tell us how one of the Kroo canoe boys who used to dive for pennies alongside the troopships in that harbour once came up on the wrong side of the ship by mistake, and how the others took advantage of his absence by tipping his box of hard-earned coins into the water and doing a mass dive for the contents.

Everyone laughed heartily at this story, I almost as loud as any. A woman in a red and white check apron had placed steaming plates of boiled potatoes, cabbage and Irish stew before Joe and me (to Joe's order). I suddenly realised I was

57

hungry as well as thirsty, and tucked in with more enthusiasm than I had ever shown before for these flavourless products of English culinary art. I wondered mildly as I did so at the understatement contained in the phrase 'a bite and a cup o' tea'; and, had I not been prevented from doing so by both Joe and Charlie, would have risked some of my funds in ordering tea or drinks all round the table. But no; I was apparently their guest – doubly so, said Charlie, for being both in their country and their café, and was to keep my money 'in case you find any Kroo canoe boys on Lake Windermere-like'.

I racked my brains for a good yarn to produce for them, and finally remembered a true story which had once been the cause of much righteous indignation amongst Sagresan mammies. The lorry drivers appreciated it, I think; for, like Charlie's tale about the Kroo boys, it illustrated the price we paid for Western 'civilisation'. A woman living in Sagresa had found herself the mother of a child she did not want. As I explained to my audience, this initial situation could not have developed in African village society, where a child is soon an economic asset, not a liability, and is always regarded as a sacred and most welcome gift from the gods. However, in this case the woman in question, being partly 'civilised', had struck upon an ingenious method of getting rid of the child, a method both safe and lucrative. She had gone with the infant to one of the markets, had asked a motherly-looking mammy to hold the baby whilst she went off ostensibly to look for change to buy a bale of cloth, and so had made good her escape, taking the cloth and leaving the baby. My audience seemed to find the story funny, but unlikely to be true, in spite of all my protestations.

Thus did time fly past unnoticed in that genial company; and it was only in the middle of a gruesome tale of Charlie's about the embarrassment of two thieves who had stolen a van in which he was conveying a corpse to a mortuary, that

I realised that if I was to get to Keswick that day I would have to continue my journey immediately. Drivers had been going in and out of the café continuously whilst we had been there, and the faces at our table had changed more than once. Joe and Charlie however were both going only as far as Carlisle that evening, and seemed to feel they had plenty of time to spare. When I expressed some anxiety about reaching Keswick before nightfall, Joe at once suggested that I spend the night with a friend of his in Carlisle, and promised to find a driver to take me into Keswick first thing in the morning, so that my programme of touring would not be upset. I was only too glad to accept this suggestion; and in a little while we took our leave of Charlie and the little café, climbed into the truck and swung out into the road once more.

I found it very difficult to express my gratitude to Joe for the experience of meeting his 'chums' in that humble roadside hut. So much of my future career was to depend on my ability to understand and establish contact with men of no greater education in my own country. I was gratified to find myself capable of being absolutely at ease in their company, and with similar experiences and stories to exchange with them. One hears so much about the gap between the intellectuals of Africa and the unlettered peasant or town dweller there whose vote at the polls is decisive. It is easy to conclude that, as in the Britain of Disraeli's day, 'two nations' are emerging in Africa, with little in common. It was reassuring for me to discover so early, and so pleasantly, that all this was much more a matter of attitudes than of education. Given a sufficiently strong motive for doing so, it was surprisingly easy to feel both interested and interesting in the company of people whose intellectual experiences were very different from one's own, and whose race and social background were even more so. I think it was this episode which helped me more than anything else to seek to cultivate the

C

art of 'being all things to all men', and of deliberately seeking that point of common interest which I believed lay hidden somewhere between myself and every individual I met.

I spent that night comfortably with Joe's friend in Carlisle, and the next morning a newsagent's van drove me out to Keswick. The hostel was not open to members until early evening, but the Warden agreed to keep my rucksack for me so that I could carry out my plan of doing a little climbing and of exploring the lakeside that day. The climbing I very soon decided was too much like hard work, rucksack or no rucksack. The slopes of Mount Skiddaw were much too steep for my liking, and the view improved only too gradually. In the end I decided that the African respiratory tract was not constructed for mountain climbing; and, after having regained my breath, I returned to road level at a leisurely pace. After all, I consoled myself, Lakes Bassenthwaite and Derwentwater might just as well be seen separately as together.

After a meal of bread and peanut butter (the latter was now my last gastronomic link with home, and I ate it on all possible occasions), I went off in search of Lake Derwentwater. Stretches of water against a background of hills had always fascinated me, and I was anxious to see if I could recreate a similar perspective here. I thought of the view back at home from Governor's Beach, whose long, curving golden crescent was set against a magnificent backdrop of dark green. I wanted to look across Derwentwater at Skiddaw, and to get the mountain to form a contrast in tone, colour and dimension with the glassy blue water. I felt like an artist composing a picture in my own imagination, as I made my way to the water's edge; except that I hoped eventually to see the picture I had conceived, not on flat canvas, but in its proper dimensions.

After a little searching I found the vantage point I believed I sought – a tiny headland jutting out from the western shore of the lake, and which commanded an excellent view across it. A few yards from the end of this headland there stood an old beech, and as I reached it with a view to seeking a place to sit, I found I had been forestalled. Sitting on a boulder at the foot of the tree, with her back to its gnarled trunk, was an English girl (as I took her to be), whose long, fair hair fell in carefully arranged tresses to her shoulders, and who wore a red pullover, a tartan kilt, and a triangular-shaped scarf thrown loosely over the shoulders. Her back was toward me; but as I stopped, hesitating as to what I should do, she turned; and revealed a face of such striking appearance that I found myself momentarily robbed of the power to do anything but stare.

It is difficult to describe that face in detail, that face whose image, during the course of the next few months, was to fill all my waking hours and many of my sleeping ones as well. Since arriving at King's, I had met very many English women students, had studied with them, danced with them, and seen many of them come to the Club on Leazes Terrace as guests of the colonial students there, to parties or to a meal. But I had often thought to myself and remarked to others that, their wardrobes apart, there was nothing our girls back at home need fear in competition with these. So often I had heard bitter complaints from our girls that we menfolk in Britain seemed to find British girls so much more attractive, that we did not hesitate to break long-standing promises, and even to disregard clearly expressed parental wishes, in order to make foreigners our wives. As a result the matri-monial market in Sagresa had become increasingly filled with frustrated old maids, who regarded every new foreign bride with thinly veiled hatred. I do not think that until I met Greta that day by Derwentwater these circumstances had been the subject of more than a few minutes of casual thought on my part. I had never been tempted to generalise about African and European girls, perhaps because I had never felt really attracted to a girl, African or European. I had sometimes even wondered whimsically whether this fact would have led my Dapo instructors to regard me as a success or a failure.

As the calm blue eyes looked me full in the face across a distance of perhaps five yards, I felt excited, and, as it were, under some strange spell. She on her part did not seem in the slightest disconcerted by the sudden appearance of a negro who must have seemed to her for the moment as being either extremely ill-bred, or else certifiably insane. She opened her lips as if to speak, but apparently thought better of it; for she merely continued to return my gaze steadily, and, now, a little amusedly, I fancied. But the slight movement had broken the spell, and I succeeded at last in finding my tongue. 'Good morning,' I stuttered. 'Please accept my apologies for the intrusion.'

'Good morning,' she said in a low, clear voice. 'It was you who surprised me, you know, not I you; so you have no excuse for being so completely taken aback.' I thought, nevertheless, that I detected a note of relief in her voice that I had not turned out to be an escapee from the local jail.

I laughed nervously, but my own composure was returning rapidly, and with it an infinitely pleasurable sensation of discovery. I believe that at first this sensation was purely the joy of having found someone else who seemed ready to talk freely to me. But very soon, it was that face I was examining in detail. The nose was small, the lips impeccably painted, the chin firm, and the complexion of great delicacy and smoothness. The cheekbones were a little too high; but this merely gave character to the features, and drew attention to the limpid blue eyes which had first arrested me, and which seemed now to be regarding me with frank curiosity.

'I am very sorry for my rudeness,' I assured her again, 'but one does not come across a charming Lady of the Lake every day of one's life, you know.'

She lowered her eyes at once and blushed very slightly, turning her face away as she did so. I had the unpleasant feeling that our meeting was about to end, that a rainbow had begun to fade. 'I see I am putting myself even more at fault now,' I added hastily; 'May I take my leave?'

I awaited the answer to the question breathlessly. It was a few moments in coming. I was just debating whether I was not being told mutely to prove that I had some manners left by going away as quickly and as quietly as possible, when she turned back to face me again. Her colour was normal once more, and she herself perfectly composed. 'Where did you learn to speak English so well?' she asked.

"At last I have my mandate to move forward," I thought; and did so, eventually to sit on a stone a few feet away from her. 'In school in Songhai. That's in West Africa. It's a British colony,' I added hastily. 'Many people speak English in the big towns there, you know.'

'I didn't. My home is in Pretoria.' I noticed that as she said this she looked at me intensely, almost anxiously. I disguised my surprise, and merely added in as level a tone as I could, 'Then that makes us both Africans. Small world, isn't it?'

She smiled a little sadly. 'There's more difference than that of pigment between a West African and a South African, I'm afraid.'

'Not fundamentally, you know,' I insisted staunchly, 'in spite of all that *apartheid* doctrinaires may say.' I was relieved at having found so soon some topic of conversation which was of mutual interest and virtually inexhaustible.

'There are many white South Africans who do not believe in *apartheid*, and I am one of them. Some, in fact, have fled the Union because of it.' This forthrightness of hers was one of the qualities I was to learn to admire most. There was

63

never any attempt to dissimulate or play for time. As much as could modestly be revealed of her opinions emerged very quickly. 'That is not to say that there are not very powerful historical reasons behind *apartheid*,' she added.

'I am afraid your Prime Minister is easily the most hated man in Africa,' I said. 'No one there is interested in finding out about historical reasons. All we know is that he wants to keep people of our race separate from people of yours, because he believes you are superior to us. As a result harmless Dutch visitors to West Africa have been attacked, and a bishop with a Dutch name has had to seek police protection. It is a popular prophecy at home that the first war a United States of Africa would have to fight would be against the Union of South Africa.'

She was silent for a long while after I had said this. It was a perfect summer's day, with hurrying white clouds reflected against the blue sky in the still waters of the lake, and a slight breeze stirring the leaves of the beech overhead. A fish plopped softly nearby, and across near the further bank a yacht leaned lazily over as if to look more closely at its own image.

'That's a terrible thing to say,' she said suddenly, almost explosively. 'Racial hatred is wicked, whoever shows it and against whomsoever it is directed.' She turned to face me squarely. 'My people are Boers. If they saw me talking to you now, even if they did not hear what I was saying, they would flog me. I have come to realise that they are hopelessly prejudiced in their opinions about the mental capacity and cultural achievement of your people – but that is because I have come to know many other African students in London University. But don't you see that the kind of thing you have just said only helps to convince my people that the two races cannot and ought not to live together?'

'I am sorry; I was thoughtless.' I looked up at her and our eyes met for a moment or two. She seemed so earnest about convincing me of the wickedness of the attitude I had described so flipppantly, that my words now seemed, in retrospect, those of a bitter, hate-filled racialist. 'Most of the peoples of West Africa are fundamentally peace-loving and tolerant,' I tried to make amends, 'but relatively few of them have ever spoken to a white person on equal terms as you and I speak now. That is probably the reason for all the trouble. You need be in no doubt as to my own personal views on the subject.'

'Those do not matter as much as the views of the majority of your people, ill-informed or not,' she answered at once. Then, in a sudden change of tone, 'I cannot really believe that a school in West Africa is wholly responsible for the fact that we understand each other so well. Are you a student too?'

And so, for what must have been a very long time, we discovered more and more about each other. Her parents, who had been wealthy farmers, had died when she was a child. She had come with her brother and his friend, both students in London like herself, to spend a week at a Keswick hotel. The two men had gone climbing on Helvellyn, which was not her idea of enjoying the beauty of the lakes; so she had brought a novel out by the lakeside for the day. The mock terror with which I scanned the nearest shrubs and trees on learning all this lit merriment in the wide blue eyes. 'It's all right, they don't follow me about to protect me from wolves – or from Britain's coloured population,' she laughed. 'They know by now that I've got a mind of my own, and that to try to thwart me does more harm than good.' She stopped, as if hesitating. Then suddenly, 'Look here, why not meet Jan and Friedrik some time this week? I am not sure whether it will work, as *they* have got pretty set ideas too, both of them. But you see they have never been able to bring themselves to make the effort to talk to someone like you as man to man, and perhaps this is my big chance to get them to change their ideas. If you, talking to them alone quietly for an hour or two, cannot convince them that there are some people of your colour who are in every sense educable, no one ever will. Would you like to try?'

It was this question which, for some reason or other, made me once more intensely conscious not of her race or nationality, but of her looks. The first vivid impression I had had of these had momentarily merged into a general sense of contentment and well-being in her company, a happy appreciation of the fact that we seemed to share at least some views in common. But her anxious question shattered the composite picture of which I had been feeling myself so happy and natural a part, and isolated her, its centre, from all else. The existence of others all round us became suddenly a matter for more than a joking glance into the nearest shrubs; and the possibility that either now or after the meeting with my prospective converts, she and I might have to part for good, became suddenly and painfully real. I had found very great happiness during those brief moments, and suddenly realised I might lose it soon.

'If you feel there's a chance of my doing some good, I'll certainly try,' I collected my thoughts sufficiently to say. 'But more than anything else, I shall welcome the opportunity of seeing you again and – and – learning more about your country,' I ended lamely. I suddenly remembered my first, impetuously flattering words to her, and regretted them. She seemed to guess my thoughts.

'You'll be careful just how you put things, won't you, both on racial topics – and on everything else.' I found it difficult to decide how to interpret the quick, oblique look she gave me as she said this. I believe now that she had from the beginning grave doubts as to whether her spur-of-the-moment invitation to me to meet the other two was a wise step. Her motives, as she had said, were merely to seek to broaden the racial horizons of her brother and his friend, by bringing them into contact with an African who was well educated. The desire to see me again for the mere pleasure of my company weighed very little, if at all, in her mind at this stage; of that I am positive. With me it was otherwise, and I regarded the meeting with the two men as merely a convenient opportunity to see her again, and to get to know her better.

'I promise,' I said, 'that I will be the soul of discretion.'

'My lunch will be waiting at the hotel.' She rose as she spoke, and smoothed her tartan and tidied her hair. She was a little less than average in height, but otherwise of proportions which, to my eyes at least, appeared faultless. The heavily pleated skirt, swinging with every movement she made, emphasised the slim waist.

'I've got some delicious peanut-butter sandwiches here, you know,' I said, with rather more earnestness than I had intended. Again there was the clear, spontaneous laugh.

'No, thank you. I am sure a healthy young man on a hiking tour here will need all the peanut-butter sandwiches he can carry; even if, like me, he does prefer looking at mountains to climbing them. But come to the bar of the Royal Keswick after dinner this evening, and I'll make the introductions.' She had already gathered her bag and book, and turned down the path. 'Bye-bye, until then.'

'One moment, please. It's easier to introduce people if you yourself know their names,' I called as casually as I could. I held out my hand with mock formality. 'Kamara; Kisimi Kamara.'

'How absent-minded of me!' She had stopped and turned. 'I am Greta, Greta Hals. Jan is my brother, and Friedrik Hertog my fiancé.'

And with that she was gone.

CHAPTER SIX

THE BAR of the Royal Keswick was not nearly as forbidding as I had imagined it might be. The chairs and stools were occupied by many customers who were obviously not hotel guests, and the air was filled with that odour, peculiar to the English pub, which is a mellow, rich blend of furniture polish, stale tobacco smoke, and alcohol fumes. Through the haze I had to peer with ebbing courage for several seconds before I was able to discern any female forms at all. I had become acutely conscious of the curious eyes turning in my direction in increasing numbers, before I saw Greta at the far side of the room.

I suppose any person in full possession of his five senses would have thought twice before keeping this particular appointment. After all, as I have already admitted, I was going to the Royal Keswick not to make converts to my racial views, but simply to see Greta again. And I now knew her to be engaged to someone who, at the best of times, had little use for men of my race. But then when a man has finally persuaded himself that he is falling in love, I suppose he is, to a greater or lesser extent, losing control of his sense of reasoning. His actions become less rational, more impulsive, and certainly less circumspect.

So I had retrieved from the bottom of my rucksack the pair of now somewhat rumpled grey flannel trousers which I had placed there for churchgoing. (Sagresan society, of course, would have been scandalised at the suggestion of worshipping God in flannels, but I felt that my offence would have been worse had I done so in corduroys.) I had ironed them carefully, and had drawn over them a lumber-jacket which I had brought along in case I encountered any cold nights. I think I looked fairly respectable, and that it was my skin and not my dress that drew the curious looks.

Greta was alone, and I sensed at once that something was wrong. She was drinking cider, and I ordered the same. It was only when I was served, and the interest my entry had aroused had begun to subside, that she referred to the absence of the two men. 'Jan will be joining us later, but Friedrik will not be coming. I am afraid he disapproves heartily of the whole idea.'

I neither felt nor showed any undue perturbation at this news. On the contrary, I deceived myself that I had won a signal victory over Friedrik already.

'Never mind,' I said. 'That is hardly likely to precipitate the end of the world.'

'No, but it is very important to me that you two should meet and that you should shake him out of his set ideas. He completes his course and returns home in four weeks' time, and then the chance will have passed for ever, perhaps.'

'You're worrying about having to marry him unconverted, aren't you?'

'Yes. Exactly.' Again the full blue eyes were looking at me direct and unflinching, as if to tell me that if I was expecting anything less than candour from her, I was wasting my time.

'Just how bigoted is he?'

'Intensely. His father was cruel to the natives on his farm, who hated him and his family like poison. But neither side could afford to do without the other. The natives used to drop lighted matches into the mailbox on the farm gate-post. Then one evening they dropped one down the petrol filler of his father's car. The old man was taking a nap in the back seat and the explosion crippled him for life. Friedrik caught the first native he could find, beat him to within an inch of his life, and left him to die in the blazing sun. Friedrik was hauled before the courts, where it was proved his victim had not been responsible for the outrage against his father. Friedrik was fined heavily. His father died a year later, and there's no doubt that the wounds and shock shortened his life. Those responsible were never found. So you see there can be as good 'historical reasons' for one man's racial bitterness as for a nation's.'

The account had shocked me deeply, and I was silent for a long while. It had been so easy, up to that point, and so convenient, to think of the racial question in South Africa purely in terms of moral black and white; and to get this terrible glimpse of its vicious complexity was an experience at once painful and disarming. In spite of myself, fantastic pictures of a small minority of white men at bay in the centre of a closing, threatening circle of bloodthirsty black men swam in bad focus across the screen of my imagination. I must have shuddered visibly, for when I looked up at my companion she was staring at me with an expression of concern, as if fearing that the effect of her words on me might have been too brutal. When our eyes met, she smiled and sheepishly, feebly, I returned the smile and took refuge in a long draught of cider. Then, on a sudden impulse, I put down my glass, leaned forward, and covered her hand on the table with mine. 'Take me up to their room now, and let me see what I can do,' I said.

Her hand turned in mine and, for a brief moment, gripped it. 'That was something I was frankly terrified of suggesting first; but which I should like us to try, for my own selfish reasons,' she smiled.

Somehow I felt within myself that my second victory over him must be won now or never, and that it would be decisive in Greta's eyes. Whatever her intentions, that touch, following close on the look of concern I had seen in her eyes earlier, set my hopes rocketing illogically and my pulse racing madly again. I was now looking forward to the encounter with the person I was rapidly convincing myself was my sworn personal foe.

'Come on,' I said eagerly.

She rose. 'This way.'

The next moment we were knocking at the door of a room in which a voice was raised in some passionate argument whose words we could not distinguish. There was a snarled 'Come in!' and I followed Greta into a well-appointed room, against the mantelpiece of which there leaned an unusually tall man, heavily built, sallow, and obviously ruffled. Above the back of an armchair drawn up to the fire protruded another man's head. I was sufficiently sure of myself to be able to take in many other details in the moment of stunned silence which followed our entry: the cloud of lazily rising blue tobacco smoke above the scalp of the second occupant of the room; the framed portrait of Greta on the mantelpiece close by the elbow of the other; the books and magazines scattered in profusion on tables and chairs.

Something in his companion's face must at last have caught the attention of the occupant of the chair, for the scalp suddenly disappeared, and a curious face emerged round one side of the armchair.

'Hello, boys. I've brought Mohammed to the mountain.'

There was no sign of strain at all in Greta's voice. She was either taking the whole business as a huge joke, or was possessed of incredible sang-froid. For a second or two longer, silence returned taut and quivering into the room.

'That's damn well the craziest thing anybody ever did,' said the man at the mantelpiece suddenly. He had, after all, had a slight start on the other in the struggle to recover his breath. 'If that's your idea of a joke, Greta, we are not amused; and I suggest that you and the rest of your comic act take yourselves off the stage at once.'

'But it was not intended to be a joke, Friedrik.' And now, for the first time, I could hear the ring of anxiety in her voice.

'I really did want you to meet Mr Kamara, and you know *why*. Yet you refused, it seemed to me, quite unreasonably. So when he asked whether he might not come here to see you I jumped at the chance. I never dreamed you would take it like this.' She threw me a quick glance over her shoulder, and I imagined I saw fright in her eyes. When I looked at Friedrik again I could see why. He was looking at me and his eyes were smouldering with hate.

'I told you this afternoon that I did not come six thousand miles to hobnob with niggers whom I kicked in the dust back at home.'

'Friedrik! You can't say things like that, man!' interposed the other man quickly.

'I don't care a damn. That girl there is supposed to be engaged to me, and if she won't learn the soft way that this type of thing – "*Mr* Kamara" and all that – just won't do for us, she's got to learn the hard way. You heard her this afternoon talking about him as if he was her bosom friend, and she's still at it now. Perhaps a bit of plain speaking will help all of us to find out what our true place is.'

The word 'nigger' is one deeply resented by all Africans who know it. Nothing will deprive us of our self-restraint so rapidly as the use of it, whether by an adult or, as so often, by an unmannerly English child. I felt my temper rising rapidly. There was only one thing to be done, and quickly.

'I have enough respect for the presence amongst us of a lady not to help *you* to your true place with my fists, Mr Hertog. You have insulted me deeply and deliberately, without the slightest provocation on my part, and before we were even introduced. I am, I assure you, only too glad to take my leave of a person of ill-breeding.' I turned to go; then found I had enjoyed saying this much, and could not resist the temptation to practise my English rhetoric a little further. I added at the door, 'If you will allow me, I shall be only too pleased to expose any further defects you may have at a time and place of your choosing. You may, however, rest assured, sir, that, once I have knocked you down in the dust, *I* shall not stoop to kick you whilst you are there. Good night, Mr Hertog.'

Feeling unaccountably elated, I passed quickly out of the hotel, and along the few hundred yards of roadway which separated the Royal Keswick from my Youth Hostel. Almost with relief, I glanced round at the faces and simple furnishings which, at first strange and curious, had already become familiar. That is the great merit of Youth Hosteling, as I was to have plenty of opportunity to discover once more; it is a way of life in which no one could help making friends and gaining wider horizons of human experience. You learned to do things you never dreamed perhaps you could do so well – cook, chop wood, clean house, sleep in a cocoon of a bag and a buzz of conversation. You met people who never would have come your way otherwise – like the harmless old eccentrics whom, in spite of their shorts and open-necked shirts, we should have described in Sagresa as having one foot in the grave and the other having no business out.

As I lay on my bunk with hands linked under my head, such thoughts formed a blurred background against which something obtruded insistently – an irrational sense of achievement, as if I had slain an enemy or won the hand of some fair maid. Neither Greta nor Hertog as such occupied my thoughts; and I had the curious sensation of thinking of them both more as characters in a novel which I had just closed than as two real persons with whom I had that day come into contact in a manner emotionally charged to a very high degree.

Suddenly I realised the Warden was at the side of my bunk. 'Some folk from the Royal Keswick want to see you. Now mind you don't keep them here too long. It's getting late.'

My vague thoughts seemed to snap abruptly into focus,

and I rose hurriedly and walked onto the decklike veranda which ran along one side of the hostel, overlooking the river. Greta and her brother came forward quickly toward me. It was Jan who spoke first. 'We felt we had to apologise to you tonight for Friedrik's behaviour. Greta says you know at least part of the story behind his attitude; but still he has never behaved so devilishly toward a complete stranger before, at least not outside the Union. It's also partly because it was Greta who was involved in the whole business with you, that he went off the deep end like that. He is almost lunatic sometimes in his jealousy over her. In any case I wanted to tell you how very sorry Greta and I feel about what happened.'

I think it is true to say that Africans, as a race, are easy-going and not given to spite. The hated term 'nigger' had bitten me like a snake at the time; but already the pain of it had eased off sufficiently to make me feel genuinely embarrassed in the face of my visitors. Greta had not spoken yet, but was clearly under considerable emotional strain. She looked tensely across the river and when she did once look straight at me I could see, even in the dim light, that she had been crying. I could only at first guess at what had happened in the room from which I had made my somewhat histrionic exit, but I was not to be kept in complete ignorance on that point for much longer.

'Please do not apologise any further. I assure you that I do not bear any grudge at all against anyone for what happened.' There was a moment's awkward pause. I had lied, of course.

'Will you have lunch with us tomorrow at the hotel?' Jan spoke heavily, and then added quickly, 'Friedrik won't be there. He is moving to another hotel in the morning.'

I glanced at Greta. It was clear that the invitation to me had been agreed on between them beforehand. 'Please!' she said in a voice far from steady, but which sounded almost pleading. It was so difficult to identify her now with my Lady of the Lake of that morning, or to realise that I had only met her twelve hours before. But the thought of how she had looked then flooded back to me with unsettling force, drowning the memory of all else that had happened that day.

'Thank you very much. I should be delighted,' I said, and meant it deeply.

A moment later they had gone and I was alone. For a long time I gazed down at the rippling waters which caught the pale moonlight and threw it back in broken silver rays. I realised, soberly and without undue alarm, that I had conceived a strong affection for a white South African girl whom I had known only for a few hours, and who was engaged to be married to a man who hated me and my race bitterly. I saw clearly that in accepting this second invitation to see her again I was deliberately taking another step across the ford of a stream the depths of which I did not know, and the currents and eddies in which I had had no opportunity to study. The danger I was flirting with threatened not only my person but, if my dreams materialised, my whole career also. It was partly because when I examined those dreams now at leisure they appeared so fanciful, that I decided to go on at all with my dreaming. After all, I finally persuaded myself, what is a holiday for if not for the indulgence of one's dreams? If I can derive a few hours of harmless satisfaction from the company of a girl who attracts me, and from contemplating what in more sober moments I might realise to be unattainable – well, why shouldn't I?

So I dismissed from my mind all thought of impending danger, turned in, and slept deeply and refreshingly.

The next day was another of those rare occurrences in the English summer – a day of almost unbroken sunshine, light breeze, and slow, wispy clouds wreathing a sky of almost royal blue. My chores at the hostel were soon done, and I packed my rucksack in readiness for the move I knew I must make that day to my next hostel. I wished to leave Keswick immediately after my lunch appointment; and, as I knew that the hostel was normally closed all day, decided to ask Jan if he would store my burdensome rucksack in his room at the hotel, whilst I went off for a walk along the Derwent valley with a copy of the 'Lyrical Ballads' for companion. Curiously, in the broad light of day, I felt far less regret at the thought of leaving Keswick and with it the company of Greta than I had done last night. I found Jan in the lounge, and he readily agreed to keep the bag for the morning. He had now entirely recovered his good humour; and we exchanged a few pleasantries. I noted with growing pleasure that he was completely at ease with me.

I declined his invitation to stay for a drink, and was just about to leave when Greta entered. She came smilingly across to us immediately; and I saw that she too had thrown off the worried look of the previous evening. I had again that sensation of coming unexpectedly upon a most remarkable *objet d'art*, perfectly conceived in movement and in speech, as in feature and proportion. She reminded me about the luncheon engagement, and asked what the 'Lyrical Ballads' were doing under my arm at this time of day. I explained my plans for the morning; and, almost impetuously I thought, Greta suggested that her brother and herself might join me. I felt same delectable excitement rising in me as I had experienced when I first touched her hand. But Jan's tone was distinctly surprised.

'Really, Greta, Mr Kamara may not want our company all morning as well as at lunch. Besides, don't forget I was out all day yesterday, and may like to laze about today.'

'Please allow him to speak for himself, Jan.' I suddenly realised that she must be older than he was. 'I am sure he is ingenious enough to find a plausible excuse for putting us off if he does not want our company, and is sensible enough to say so if he does.' A look of mischief shone in her eyes.

'I shall be honoured, I assure you.' It was becoming more difficult every moment to keep up the effort of carefully chosen words and gestures with this girl. 'Wordsworth is exceedingly dull heard in one's own voice.'

'Then you two will have to go alone. I'll stay and make sure of that corner table.' He did not sound in the slightest annoyed, though I came to the conclusion later that he must have hoped secretly that his sister would have baulked at the thought of strolling alone with me along the valley of the Derwent. But she had already turned away.

'All right! Shan't be long.'

That morning was the happiest in my life up till then. We walked together a long way, reading to each other in turn, or talking of our respective countries, their differing ways of life, their problems, what in them gave us pleasure and what did not. Occasionally we would stop at a point where some particularly attractive vista of water, fields and woods offered, and we found a shared instinct for absorbing to the full the enjoyment to be derived from these scenes. We could both, I think, sense then that in drawing thus closer to the loveliness of the day and the country, we were also drawing closer to each other. On one occasion as, silent for a few moments, we walked softly along a mossy path in the shade of a shrubbery which bordered the river, the soft ululant cry of a bird sounded with startling clarity from a tree not ten feet from us. We both looked up, but the foliage was too thick; and as our eyes met and we laughed it was difficult to look away again. That plaintive call seemed somehow charged with a significance for us, even though we might not wish to stop and discover it. It was our second moment of mutual embarrassment in each other's company, and our laughter ended a little hollowly. But in a moment the mood had passed, and we were once more abandoning ourselves to the plain, unspoiled pleasures which the sights and sounds of nature, and the thoughts and language of the poet, held in store for us.

This was the first of very many such walks during the course of the next fortnight. There was no turning back now. Greta and I travelled to a daily rendezvous by bus from her hotel and my hostel each day, to explore the Lake District and discover each other. She told me that Friedrik had broken off their engagement the very evening of our first encounter. Now finally convinced that her attitude and his to the problem of race were so fundamentally divergent as to preclude all possibility of a successful married life in the Union, she had refused to take back the ring he had afterwards tried to return to her. I realised as she spoke that she had turned to me for the companionship, for the sharing of views and experience, which Friedrik had been able to give her only imperfectly. As if under a helpless spell, I watched what I had judged the impossible happen. Every sign in her of a growing affection for me intensified my ardour intolerably. In the background of my blurred vision I was vaguely conscious of the presence of Jan, and of his giving us ever clearer indications that he disapproved of the turn events were taking. My career, which I knew would be imperilled if I married without permisison from the Songhai Government, loomed much larger than did Jan in my thoughts during those passionate weeks. But neither of us dared raise so towering a problem as marriage.

To Friedrik I do not think I gave another thought. We believed him to be still in the neighbourhood, but saw nothing of him; and, after the first day or two little of Jan either. I know now that what Greta and I were experiencing was a fond infatuation, not love. We were both young, both physically attractive; and, what was more, were each going through such an experience for the first time. I knew of course that persons of different race did sometimes find themselves caught in this strange magnetic field, stronger because it derived from opposites. Had the emotional force pulling us together been less strong and less suddenly applied, we might have weighed with more care the dangers to which we were exposing ourselves; or at least might have thought it prudent to allow our feelings to be tested in the slow crucible of time. Instead we threw caution to the winds, made the most extravagant promises of enduring devotion to each other, and rose light and unworried in flights of quite uncontrolled imagination over every other consideration. I had thus far forgotten my father's final message to me, and the anxious hopes which centred on my career

Then one day she brought two rugs instead of one, and we slept together through the balmy summer night, in the shadow of a haystack. And as dawn broke and passion cooled, reason returned stealthily. Two weeks of mounting intoxication, then a sip of nectar, and the effect was bittersweet, cloying, sobering. We lay awake through that slow dawn, just thinking, not speaking at all. I thought of my Africa, of my little girl in the red beads, bathing and singing in the rain. She thought of her Africa, a very different Africa, but no less jealous and possessive than mine. I know she thought of it, although she never told me.

That evening we had a quiet dinner together at her hotel. But we had no appetite. We both sensed a different relationship, and were seeking words with which to define it clearly to ourselves. We wanted to talk intimately, alone – perhaps that would help. We each felt a strange hurt deep inside, and were seeking balm.

We left our meal unfinished and went out. Linked arm in arm, we stepped from the brightly lit hotel porch into the darkness of the road. As we did so, I heard the engine of a car revving up noisily in a corner of the car park; but we were in no frame of mind to give a second thought to such trivialities. The sound grew rapidly louder; but no car lights were visible, so we did no more than stop in the middle of the roadway, even then more curious than alarmed, our eyes still not fully adjusted to the dark. Then, with shocking suddenness, two powerful headlights were switched blindingly on not more than thirty feet from where we stood. Completely dazzled, and transfixed with horror, for a moment we could only watch them surging forward. Then I made a frantic, desperate attempt to drag Greta out of danger. As I did so the approaching vehicle swerved, screaming, inexorable, in the very direction we had moved. The angry, glaring discs of white light seemed to leap directly at us; I heard a terrified gasp from the girl at my side; and then my consciousness was blotted out by a cloud of nausea, pierced by jabbing flashes of excruciating pain.

CHAPTER SEVEN

WHEN I REGAINED consciousness late the next evening I was in a hospital ward whose whiteness seemed to be in my nostrils as much as in my eyes. My left leg was completely numb below the knee; but as memory swept the swirling clouds away with painful slowness and full consciousness returned, my first words were a frantic, burbled inquiry about Greta. A white-clad figure standing by the bedside looked down at me with eyes of infinite pity, but without speaking. Words could hardly have spoken more plainly than did that look, and the clouds of nausea and merciful oblivion rolled back over the sky of my consciousness.

My life hung on a thread for a week. When I knew it was safe, I developed an all-consuming lust to avenge Greta's death. At first I was able to find an outlet for my emotion by making statements of a highly passionate nature to a grave police officer who was at my bedside with pencil and note-book whenever the doctors allowed him. He told me that I could be sure that everything had been done to trace the vehicle and driver responsible for 'the incident'. When I gathered that 'everything' consisted in taking measurements on the spot and broadcasting a 'The-driver-failed-to-stop' announcement, I bellowed and fumed incoherently, until the officer was led away from the ward by an alarmed nurse. Much later, in a calmer mood, I described to another officer how the vehicle had appeared to me deliberately to swerve toward us when we jumped away. He looked in turn shocked, incredulous, and reproachful; and then, after careful reflection, said that unfortunately as persons jumping on a tarred road did not leave tracks, it would be impossible to establish with certainty the pattern of movement which preceded 'the incident'. However, was there anyone on whose movements at the time I would like him to check?

I immediately gave him Friedrik's name, vicious spite burning in my heart. I told him too, at his request, the full tale of my relationship with Greta, her brother and Friedrik since the day I had first met them. He left me obviously more worried about my mental state than convinced that my suspicions might be justified. When I think back now on the complete absence of any hard evidence linking Friedrik with Greta's death, I wonder at the officer's willingness even to investigate as far as he did. Three days later I learned that there had been no response whatsoever to the broadcast announcement, and that no car whose tyres matched the skid marks left on the road had been identified. Worst of all Friedrik had satisfied the police that he was in a London-bound sleeper at the time, and Jan that he was dining in his digs in Earl's Court. The policeman's eyes, usually merely ferrety and restless, were now almost embarrassed with emotion, as his eyes strayed over all the paraphernalia with which modern medicine had found it necessary to festoon me. The thin lips moistened, and the tongue licked over them in a gesture which clearly betrayed his anxiety to get the distasteful business over as soon as possible. Of course, he assured me, the file in this case would not be closed while the identity of the driver and vehicle remained unestablished. Until there was further evidence on the matter, however, the police would have to proceed on the assumption that I had been injured and Greta had lost her life as the result of a tragic accident. They would ascribe the accident to an unidentified driver moving at reckless speed out of the car park, and delaying to switch on his lights. Investigations would, however, continue. . . .

And with a wheezy sigh of relief, and a stentorian clearing of the throat, my visitor bade me good day and hurried away from my bedside.

Thus began for me a twelve-month-long hell of the deepest mortification. With the exit of that police officer from my ward, the blackness of utter dejection and hopelessness swept in on me, the conviction that a terrible crime had been committed which there was no one to unmask; that an evil monster had stalked and slain, unrecognised and unchallenged. I had a relapse. My reserves of nervous and physical energy, so urgently needed to supplement the skill of the surgeons and the patience of the nurses, were sapped by terrible, exhausting nightmares and hallucinations. I had to be isolated, and a psychiatrist consulted. For weeks, I learned afterwards, it was feared that my mind might have suffered permanent injury. Then, having sunk gradually all autumn and, throughout the winter, wavered along on a tenuous thread, the graph of my health began slowly to climb with the coming of spring. As the air grew warmer and the trees outside my window dressed their bare limbs with bursting buds; as the songs of the birds in the early morning gained in volume, variety and cheerfulness, and the devoted nurses who tended me seemed themselves to walk with a lighter, more hopeful step; my will returned to me, and I caught the universal spirit of renascence. With the will to get better came the strength for the task. I began reading letters from Sagresa and elsewhere which had lain unopened in my closet for months, and assuring all who cared to listen that, God willing, I should be up and about that summer. To my parents, who had been kept acquainted with all that had happened by the matron, I wrote a long, carefully composed epistle, making no mention of Greta. I told them that as soon as I was discharged I would resume my studies, and that I would surely return to them all one day.

My letter was more confident than were my private

thoughts on the matter. I had decided to use every penny I could lay hands on in trying to establish a case of murder against Friedrik. I was hoarding all money received from home and from my scholarship to engage the services of a good criminal lawyer in the case. But my parents' heartbreak had trembled so passionately even through the stilted English phrases of the letter writer, that I could not bear to prolong their anguish longer. And in a few days' time I received an air-letter from them in return which showed that they had taken my letter at its word; and had once more resumed their patient and confident vigil for my ultimate return.

One day Samuel, who had already made several unsuccessful attempts to find me, reached my bedside. He wept like a baby on seeing me again. But I could not bring myself to tell even him about Greta. I had launched out on a secret and intensely personal crusade, and was determined to fight it through alone. Samuel returned to Birmingham reassured. Warmhearted and loyal as ever, he had been quite prepared to give up a term's work to stay near me, had it proved to be necessary.

On the day in early summer I was discharged, it was with only five guineas in my pocket. I had used the whole of my scholarship grant for the following term to pay the fee of a firm of solicitors, who had merely advised me to drop the case as hopeless. The rest of my savings had gone in medical expenses. I boarded a train for Liverpool, the only big city I knew outside Newcastle. After an agonising mental struggle, I had decided that the police and lawyers were right. The Greta episode was finally closed. I had to find work, both to earn money and to erase memories. I chose Liverpool because there I would be nearer to Samuel. But I was confident also that in so big a city I could surely earn enough to pay for at least the first term of my resumed studies, and so save the scholarship I would lose if I failed to re-enroll. I found a cheap boarding-house, and began job-hunting. With a pleasant sensation of fortitude and self-dependence warm within me, I combed the streets looking out for 'Vacancy' notices, and scanned the advertisement columns of the newspapers.

It was only after three days of futile effort that I began to doubt the wisdom of what I had undertaken. I was down to my last pound, with not the slightest prospect of securing the type of moderately well-paid job for which I was looking. Only a stubborn, proud determination prevented me from falling back on the National Assistance Board. On several occasions I had answered by telephone an advertisement for a clerk, had been assured that the vacancy still existed, and on turning up for interviews had been told that it had been filled. I suppose the unexpected sight of a now distinctly shabby negro contrasted too sharply with what my voice over the telephone had led my prospective employers to expect. I was repeatedly made to feel like a tramp who had strayed into a Bond Street shop.

One evening I found that there were probably deeper reasons than reaction against the unexpected for my failure to secure employment. Wandering along a brightly lit street which led down to the arches of the overhead railway, I found a clubhouse which was packed full of coloured folk. For lack of a better way of passing the time, I entered, and was soon chatting happily with some Kroo seamen at a table in one corner. Over beers we exchanged experiences; and I soon found that they had the capacity for forgetting for the instant about all their past troubles, and extracting from the care-free present every ounce of enjoyment and fun they could, by way of anecdote, rich infectious laugher, song, drink, and dance. The place was heavy with cigarette smoke, and a tinny piano, excruciatingly out of tune, was being jazzed upon with great ferocity in one corner. Here I learned that, with the rising volume of immigation of West Indians and West Africans into Britain, popular feeling had begun to turn against offering them employment of a sort which a 'white' British subject might find himself in need of. In short, I might have to set my sights a little lower if I was in urgent need of employment.

If one had to spend one's last shillings somewhere, this was as good a place as any, I thought. I took my turn in standing drinks all round; and then, feeling pessimistic in a cheery kind of way, I made my way to my lodgings, almost penniless, but no longer quite friendless.

The next day I got my job – night watchman at a warehouse down on Regent Road. I will not try to pretend that I found it in the slightest degree congenial. Its only advantage was that, in between my half-hourly rounds of the building, I could get in a good deal of the reading of English classics which was still a passion with me. But even in summer I found the night breezes coming off the Mersey uncomfortably cold, and the weird sounds and sights of dockland in the dead of night disconcerting. Moreover there was too much noise by day in the Upper Parliament Street area where my lodgings were situated to allow me to sleep much; and I soon found myself dozing on the job. Afraid of the consequences of such lapses, I began again my search for a more suitable job. Within a week I had secured one as tally clerk in the dockside warehouse of a big firm. This was a distinct promotion, and I took up my new duties with eagerness.

I am even now surprised at the ease with which I adapted myself to tasks and surroundings which were so completely unfamiliar to me at the time. I suppose the fact that as a schoolboy at Lokko I had learned to do all sorts of menial tasks for my missionary guardians protected me from the danger of regarding manual labour as degrading. Indeed I learned to admire greatly the men who worked on those ships and in those warehouses and stores. Their language was often coarse and their manners boorish; but their hearts were good, and their loyalty both to each other and to the unwritten code of dockland behaviour and ethics was illimitable. They worked hard while on the job, and would never do anything which might get their colleagues into trouble. Above all, I could see that they took a great pride in their work, whether it was skilled or unskilled, and in doing it as quickly and as efficiently as they could.

I have often since been grateful for those weeks of work in that company. I knew the stranglehold which the white collar had established on sophisticated West African society. The Sagresa school had tried to teach each of us a trade; but, so strongly did public opinion outside the school hold the view that even a starving professional was nearer to the kingdom of heaven than the most successful artisan, that none of us took these attempts very seriously. In its own way, the caste system in the towns of West Africa was in those days as rigid and as vicious as the Hindu variety, and as unquestioned. None of us schoolboys would dream of carrying our own luggage even a few hundred yards between home and school at the beginning of term – a Fula labourer must be called for this purpose, and be given a shilling from which perhaps we could ill afford to part. But those school days were in a sense an interlude as far as I was concerned. In Liverpool I quickly re-learned the lesson I had learned in the missionary bungalow at Lokko – that there is not merely dignity, but deep satisfaction, in humble tasks performed to the best of one's ability and in pursuit of a desired objective.

Moreover, those plain, hard-living, hard-swearing men taught me to laugh at myself in a way I had never done before. I had previously assumed that to be an 'intellectual' was necessarily something entirely desirable, the sight of which would arouse envy in anyone not so favoured. But one day when a heavy fall of rain drove everyone off the quayside and kept us kicking our heels in the warehouse for half a morning, I provided the men with their biggest laugh of the week by attempting to demonstrate how wide was my acquaintance with English idiom. I had gone to the warehouse entrance to see whether there was any sign of a break in the weather. There wasn't; and, passing a group of dockers on the way back, I observed with exaggerated disgust: 'I'm thoroughly browned-off, chaps.' Fortunately for my reputation, I saw the joke almost as soon as I had produced it, and was able to join in the merriment. But in future, although I still kept my ears open for phrases and words which might enrich my vocabulary, I was more selective in my own use of English colloquialisms.

After a month I took stock of my position. I was learning, it was true, much about the Englishman, his way of life and his language, which I could have learned in no other way. But I knew that I could only complete the course of study I had begun and keep faith with my people at home, by returning to the disciplined, and expensive, studies which only the university offered. Listening to modern slang by day and reading Milton by night was all very well. But it needed only the briefest of calculations at the end of that first month to show me that in this job too I was not saving enough to pay a term's fees at King's.

That evening, for the first time since leaving the hospital, I was engulfed in another wave of deep depression. It was not the past now that buffeted me. I was able successfully to delude myself that I had forgotten all about that. My will to forget was strong, and I assumed that every level of my mind could be subjected to its strength. It was the future that now seemed so black. I might have turned to Samuel now for the financial help I knew he would at once have given me. But because I knew how much he loved me, I decided I could not. Samuel would have had to imperil his own scholarship to have been of any material help to me now. And I knew he would have done so without hesitation.

In utter dejection, I stumped down Upper Parliament Street and, hardly caring where I was going, turned into the

Cathedral. The choir was practising; it was the final chorus from the 'St Matthew Passion', music which compels the attention of even the most unmusical by its very sweep and grandeur. I found a pew and sat down, arrested. It was a double choir, probably specially assembled for a coming festival or concert; for the throaty, rich voices of women dominated the pellucid unemotional voices of the boys in the soprano and contralto parts. The tragic phrases and cadences rose and fell echoingly, and the echo seemed to find further reflection in my own heart. It was music I knew very well, as it was a favourite of the Durham College's Musical Society, whose concerts I had often attended. But now I, who normally could not bear to listen to a piece of music I knew without joining in, could only listen, mutely, ears and heart in perfect concord with Bach's mood.

As the choir reached its triumphant final chord, I became conscious that I was no longer alone in the pew. A young woman sat a few feet away from me, and a man close to her on the other side. They both looked at me curiously; and I realised that even in the subdued light of the nave I must have been betraying the powerful feelings which the music had at once echoed and intensified in me. I did not wish to make contact with strangers just then, and I found myself shying away violently from conversing with white women.

'It's wonderful music, isn't it?' The man had leaned over the girl and was clearly determined to make conversation with me. 'They are doing it on Sunday. Hope you've got your ticket all right.'

'No, I'm afraid I haven't.' I was curt because ill-at-ease.

'What a shame!' It was the woman speaking in a half-whisper. 'They are all sold out, aren't they, John?'

'Yes. You looked so completely carried away just now.' He seemed to be turning something over in his mind. 'Will you be here on Sunday – in Liverpool, I mean?'

'Yes.' I was thawing a little before the warmth of their friendliness.

The couple looked at each other for a moment.

'Look here, if you can spare a moment to come round the corner to our house I think we can find a spare ticket for you.'

I almost refused the offer; but restrained myself on reflecting that the more dejected my mood, the greater was my need for some sort of distraction. I felt almost guilty at my readiness to use such great music to so negative a purpose. But I quieted my conscience by reminding myself that, however low the price of the ticket I was about to buy, in my reduced financial circumstances I was going to pay a high price for it.

On the way to the house I also received from the couple, and accepted, an invitation to supper. Over supper, I found once more how far the individual English couple at home can depart from the national norm of reserve and uncommunicativeness. This young married couple were deeply and genuinely interested in me and in my story, and their interest evoked a ready response in me. I had soon told them pretty well all I wished to divulge as to how I had reached Liverpool from Lokko.

'Songhai,' said the man, whom I had discovered to be a young business executive in the jewellery trade. 'Where all the diamonds come from?'

'That's right,' I replied, sipping gratefully at a piping hot cup of coffee. 'But the stones travel along some pretty odd channels en route. There's a great deal of smuggling going on, you know.'

'I believe so. And impossible to check now, I suppose. The stuff is easily come by, is it?'

'Yes, all over the place, in certain districts. There's one story of a man who built a brand-new mud hut, and then had to break it down again quickly to secure for himself the stones which were sticking out of its walls everywhere. That's probably apocryphal; but the Customs people and the lawyers could tell you many truer tales of attempted smuggling. And you may be sure that for every smuggler that's caught, there are ten who are not.'

'Do help yourself to more biscuits and cheese. I don't suppose you thought of bringing a few lumps away with you in your pockets,' said my hostess.

'Lumps of what, darling? Biscuits or cheese?'

'Diamonds, stupid!'

'No, I'm afraid not,' I laughed. 'At least nothing saleable. I've got a rough stone sent me as a memento by my father just as I was sailing.'

'Ooh, may I see it? No one in John's firm is allowed to bring them home, rough or polished; and I've never seen the real thing!'

'All our staff are married to diamond-loving wives; so that particular rule of the firm's was made entirely in self-defence.'

'Horrid thing! But was I really asking too much, Mr Kamara? If so I do apologise.'

'Not at all,' I said hurriedly. I had not, it was true, shown the stone to anyone since it was given to me, mainly I think because the occasion to do so had not arisen. Also I was not sure whether in bringing into the country even a personal keepsake such as this I might not have broken some law or other. But here, in this cosy English parlour, with the flickering warmth of a good coal fire toasting my feet and my sense of loneliness and frustration momentarily dispelled, to grant a curious young housewife who had befriended me her wish seemed harmless enough. I was feeling more thoroughly at ease than I had believed I could ever be again in the company of a white girl. I experienced once more the satisfying sensation that I had succeeded completely in 'getting over' the harrowing events of the previous summer.

The stone was hanging against my chest on a silver chain. I pulled it out and held it carefully in the palm of my hand.

It felt warm, and good to hold.

'There you are! Disappointing, isn't it?' I said.

'Yes, it is, rather. I expected it to be bigger, and of course much prettier.'

'My dear girl, that pebble in our friend's hand is worth more than this house and all its contents.'

'I've never thought about its value really, to tell you the truth,' I said. 'Is it really worth all that?'

'Not as it is, of course. It would need cutting and polishing by an expert. I only deal with the administrative side of the business, and can't tell you much about the cutting and value-ing sides of it. But I'm sure you've got a small fortune there. Anyhow, since you're not interested in its commercial value, it doesn't make much odds if I'm wrong, does it?'

I did not answer for a moment. A thought had just entered my head which I found at once exciting and shocking. After a moment or two's contemplation I put it aside firmly for the time being.

'No. I suppose not,' I answered.

'I hope you won't consider it too personal if I ask you how and where you learned your English?' asked Mrs Morris.

'Not at all. We speak it as a lingua franca at home. We have many languages and many tribes; so it's just as well that English has been kept as the medium of instruction in the schools. It links us both with each other and with so much of the outside world.'

We were comfortably seated in deep leather arm chairs in front of the fire, and my hosts seemed as interested in me and my country as I was grateful for their company and the hospitality of their hearth.

'What course of studies are you following at Newcastle?'

'Reading for an English degree.'

'Enjoying it, or sickening for home? I must say when we first saw you on that pew we were certain that something was making you extremely unhappy – but thought it might be merely the effects of Bach's "tears of grief".' Morris was genuinely delighted at their success in cheering me up.

'I have my ups and downs, of course.' I changed the subject quickly. 'You know, it is fascinating to study the way in which your language has proved itself adaptable alike to the needs of different peoples, of different social classes, and of different periods of history. In Africa, for example, where developments are taking place so rapidly that modern states are being created within decades, we have put its flexibility to good use. There is an interesting form of "pidgin English" spoken all along the coast. Since it is only in recent times that anyone listened to what a man of under thirty had to say on any subject, we still use the term "big man" as synonymous with "old man". An aged beggar, in this sense, is a "bigger man" than a young Prime Minister.'

'I wonder,' said Morris, 'whether old people really prefer to be paid respect, as you do, or pensions, as we do.'

'Oh, they get the pensions as well from us, don't you worry. But not from the State; from any younger relative whose career shows even the faintest signs of making progress – and when I say relative, distance is no object. But if you are interested in the subject still, let me give you a few more examples of how we have adapted your flexible language to our needs.'

'Please do,' said Mrs Morris. 'John's pet theme is money, which can become a little tantalising for a wife who possesses none.'

My thoughts switched again to the rough stone on the table, and I found that the idea that had entered my head a few minutes ago had now hardened into a decision, without further conscious effort on my part.

I had found my most attentive audience yet, and the evening passed away quickly and pleasantly. When at last I took my leave of my kind friends, it was with a deep sense of obligation to them for much more than a concert ticket, more even than an evening's pleasant companionship.

All the way home, and for a very long time that night, I wondered why I had not thought about it before. But it is so often the things closest to us we overlook. Here was a simple solution to my most anxious problem. I felt short-lived qualms about using my father's parting gift for such a purpose. Soon there supervened the matter-of-fact admission that the wrong I would be doing my family by failing to finish my course would be immeasurably greater than the disrespect implied in realising some hard cash from my father's memento. Moreover, I had developed a genuine liking for English studies, and wished ardently to finish my course.

Thus it was that after the concert that Sunday I walked with Morris back to his home. I told him I was completely out of funds, and asked him whether he thought it might be possible to realise enough money from the sale of my stone to help to pay my way through at least one term at college.

'My dear chap, nothing would be easier. But why did you not tell us all this the other evening? We could have saved you at least two further nights of anxiety. Now listen. One of my best friends cuts and polishes these things. If you will trust me with it I'll consult him first thing tomorrow – but I'm sure it will be as easy as falling off a haystack, since we are in the trade.'

'I should like if possible to get it back eventually, or part of it, at any rate. Could it be pawned, or perhaps broken up and only part of it sold?'

'Pawning won't work,' Morris frowned. 'Most pawnbrokers are too suspicious of stuff as big as this. They won't touch it with a barge-pole. As to breaking it, I could answer your question more confidently after having shown the stone to my friend; but, assuming that all you want to keep is a small

94

fragment – as a kind of keepsake of a keepsake – I should guess it could be done without reducing the value of the remainder very much. But that's just a guess.'

Gratefully, I slipped the hard, unpromising-looking mineral into his hand. 'Call at this time tomorrow, and I'll let you know for sure.'

'Thank you so much.' My gratitude was deeply felt. 'I will.'

We parted, but I had taken only a few paces toward my lodgings when I heard him call me back.

'Incidentally, I take it that, whatever laws you broke in bringing this stone out of the country, it may now be regarded as your property, at least *de facto*?'

'I think, by common law, *de jure* too,' I said indignantly. 'The thing was found by an African on African soil which, according to our traditions, cannot be alienated. It was then given to me, and I brought it here. Whatever may be written in the latest edition of the laws, I don't see how any code of common justice, or any healthily functioning human con-science, could deny me the right to its ownership.'

Morris was a little taken aback by my vehemence. He swallowed hard. 'Oh, I'm not seriously worried about it. The stone is only suspect until it's cut and polished, and we can keep its existence to ourselves until then. After that, as I've said, it will be introduced quite openly into our normal trade channels. I merely wished to be assured that I shall be representing the situation correctly to my friend tomorrow.'

And so my father's diamond came timely to my rescue. In due course it was sold for a figure which enabled me to buy suitable presents for the Morrises, pay Morris's friend a handsome fee, return to King's College, and salt away a sub-stantial sum. And I was still left with a small fragment of the original memento. Before I left Liverpool, I remembered to enter once more the Cathedral where the clouds had first begun to lift. There I returned thanks to the God whom I had been taught from earliest childhood watched over the destinies of those who sought, to the best of their powers, to live the good life as they conceived it. Smug, no doubt; but also distinctly comforting.

CHAPTER EIGHT

My last three years at King's College passed quickly. I worked extremely hard. All colonial students had to do so to keep up with British students.

It was at this time that I had occasion to give practical expression to my friendship with Samuel. He was one of those unfortunate people who, after successfully clearing a number of academic hurdles, come to one which, try as hard and as often as they may, they cannot surmount. He had lost his scholarship because of 'unsatisfactory progress', as shown by three unsuccessful attempts at his First M.B. He had now abandoned the medical course for law, and was precariously financed by relatives and friends at home. He now reluctantly accepted as a loan most of my savings from the diamond sale. Samuel, quiet, serious-minded as ever, was showing great tenacity of purpose in continuing his studies in the face of these difficulties. He had always had an original and inventive mind, and succeeded in earning a fair amount of pocket-money by selling manufacturing and advertising ideas to commercial firms. He would show me with pride a slogan he had thought up for painting on the backs of buses: 'CAN'T OVERTAKE? YOU NEED SURE FIRE PETROL!' I had never associated him with gimmicks, but he seemed to enjoy thinking them up. He was hoping eventually to take a London law degree, but in the meanwhile was studying in Newcastle for the sake of economy, using the library of King's. We moved in together to lodgings in the Scotswood Road, and found that in this way we could live reasonably comfortably. I remember that during the first few weeks in the Scotswood Road, the evenings which he did not devote to mastering contract and tort were occupied in trying to perfect the details of another of his 'ideas', one which he claimed would enable bus companies to dispense with the services of their conductors. Each passenger was to insert his fare into a complicated little coin machine attached to the back of the seat in front. This machine would gently but automatically collapse the seat at the end of the journey to which the fare paid entitled the passenger. It all sounded very ingenious, and Samuel at any rate was convinced it would work. Moreover, he pointed out, it would deliver the *coup-de-grâce* to the dying practice of giving up your seat to the nearest lady. This particular idea was in fact eventually sold for twenty-five pounds to a bald, bespectacled, middle-aged crackpot, who rushed down to the Patent Office in London with it, and was never heard of again – done in one dark night, they said, just outside the headquarters of the Bus Conductors' Union.

However, when I completed my course successfully (securing a second class), I was glad to be able to leave my friend with enough saved from our joint resources to free him from financial anxiety for a considerable period. I did not wish to wait for the formal conferring of my degree, for a new feeling of restlessness had gripped me since receiving the news of my success in the finals. Samuel and I had both been aware of a mounting interest, during the last year together in Newcastle, in political developments back at home. We read avidly every word of the local papers which we had sent out to us, and often discussed far into the night what we considered to be the unsatisfactory progress being made by our political leaders in winning independence for Songhai, and what could be done to hasten matters up. We were now not only bursting with answers to every political problem that arose, but also cocksure about the usefulness of the contribution we could make when we returned. On our last night together, we pledged ourselves to work together as soon as possible after Samuel's return 'to free our beloved country from the shackles of imperialism and lead it into self-government'. The pledge was written down in those terms, and solemnly signed; and my copy is still with me, a very dear and cherished possession.

Thus, five years after I had first left it, I returned to my country, a little sadder and a little wiser. And it was to a very different country that the M.V. *Adonkia* was carrying me that July. I first noticed the change in the attitude of the ship's crew. The shipping company had at last come to realise that it would lose more now by alienating the African first-class passenger than by alienating his white counterpart. The balance of power in Africa was swinging irresistibly across the colour-bar, and a lot of ideas required adjusting in consequence. It was clearly a bitter pill for most of those stewards to swallow. I was amused to notice that now African passengers were receiving ungrudging and even ingratiating service on board. Moreover (an even greater transformation, in a sense) African stewards had been engaged, and were accepted perfectly naturally by their white colleagues and by white passengers alike.

The contemplation of these changes whetted even further my curiosity to get home and observe at first hand what had taken place in West Africa during those five years to overcome such deep-seated prejudices and habits. I was soon to see that developments were in motion on that continent as complex and profound as any which had overtaken a race of human beings anywhere at any time.

I landed at home to find that, during my absence, my country too had been swallowing pills – large and indigestible doses of the materialism of 'Western civilisation'. I came back to a stimulated land, pepped up into frantic, exhausting activity. It was not merely physical appearances that had altered so completely, the buildings, harbours, roads, bridges and so on; although the change here was marvellous enough.

Much more fascinating to me were the changes in the people and, I soon found, much more disturbing too. New motives for action, new attitudes toward others, were as apparent in them as in the shipping company's crews. There were new lusts too, which I did not remember being so blatantly indulged formerly – the lust for quick power, for quick riches; the unconcern as to what methods were employed in the process; the readiness to use, and even deliberately to foster, age-old inter-tribal animosities. These had now been given a terribly sharp edge, driven with the force and on the scale possible in a community which had been suddenly presented with the whole gamut of Western institutions. It was not that the African was just a nice chap, innocent and simple, who had been corrupted overnight by too intimate an association with an evil acquaintance. Rather was it that, by setting out on a deliberate policy of abandoning almost abruptly a way of life which our forebears had pursued contentedly for many centuries, and adopting that of a distant northern people, we had reached a point where we were finding it increasingly difficult to keep a foothold on anything. We were in danger of losing our sense of direction, of purpose, of faith in ourselves.

I found myself drawn helplessly (and, I may add, without any feeling of regret) into the same aimless, puzzled, befogged existence. Short-term, materialistic objectives which in a clearer atmosphere I should have recognised as quite inadequate seemed all that was worth living for. Collecting as many degrees as possible; seeing in supporting a political party or leader merely the chance to draw in time a Minister's salary of three thousand per annum; progressing as rapidly as possible up the ladder of car-ownership which stretched from the Ford Popular to the Cadillac – all around me these were the things that now mattered, and I slipped easily into the same frame of mind. There had been a great increase in wealth, most of it obtained through unlicensed diamond

comment on the same page came out in strong opposition to what it called the Nationalists' 'rape of the constitution'. The editorial was well written and lucidly reasoned; and for the first time since my return from the United Kingdom, I felt, as I read, a quick rising of irritation within me at injustice done to others of my race. The editor admitted that the South African Government was by no means the only government which pursued or condoned a policy of racial discrimination; but he pointed out that the 'disturbing' thing about the Republic was that it alone of all such countries was actually retrogressing in its racialist policy. Some other countries with a colour bar were gradually seeking to remove it – the United States, for example. There might conceivably be some which were marking time in the matter. But South Africa was actually putting the clock back, complained the editor, was acting on assumptions about the inferiority of one race to another which had been disproved twenty-five years ago.

I turned over the page. There was a picture of white police in a South African town forcily removing natives from their homes, for no other reason, the caption said, than that more elbow room was wanted for nearby white communities. The move was made twenty-four hours before the notice given had expired, so that disturbances would be avoided; and a white police officer was photographed carrying a screaming, protesting African woman to a waiting lorry. He was carrying her as if she were an animal. 'Unceremonious' or 'undignified' might have been suitable adjectives to apply to such an action in normal circumstances. Unfortunately circumstances were not normal: the struggling woman was clearly in an advanced stage of pregnancy. Underneath the photograph was a question whose deliberately brutal pun struck me like a vicious blow in the stomach: 'WHAT SORT OF FUTURE CAN THIS WOMAN EXPECT?'

As I gazed in helpless and mounting agitation at that picture I felt first of all as if all the blood were being drained out of my body. Then a blind, choking fury swept into me, clouding my senses and agitating my whole body. I cannot now tell how long I remained in that condition; but I know that when I recovered my self-control eventually, I was still trembling violently, that I felt extremely cold, and that the mosquito net seemed about to suffocate me. I extricated myself with some difficulty from it, put on a warm dressing gown, lit a cigarette, and paced my veranda – twenty-two yards long, to enable, they had said, British occupants to practise their bowling.

Events come, leave their mark on us, and pass on. Sometimes the mark is faint; but at other times it may be quite indelible, however much our memory may deceive us that the incident is forgotten. The forest stream may disappear underground for a while; but nothing can prevent it reappearing on the surface at some lower point in its course.

As I paced the veranda my footsteps seemed as drum-beats to the ceaseless, rhythmless castanets of the crickets all around me. Against the background of this doleful sound-track, vivid scenes from the last few years flashed upon my mind's taut screen: My first sight of the Sagresa cotton tree; the farewell of the girl bathing in the rain; the disillusionment of Liverpool; the fantastic dream-turned-nightmare that a carefree trip to the Lake District had brought me. No mortal could live through such a sequence of experiences and then merely shrug it off, picking up the threads of life at a point where they had been so nearly severed, without some change taking place in the pattern of that life. And yet that was precisely what I had persuaded myself that I had been successful in doing. Up to this moment, I had assumed that I was none the worse for my experience.

I was still trembling, or perhaps it was shivering; for not

all my pacing had got rid of my feeling of extreme coldness. I recognised that basically my present condition was one of irrational, furious loathing against a whole race. But over and above this emotion, there was a criss-cross of other sensations and thoughts. I caught myself wishing ardently that I had found and married the most beautiful girl in Songhai, and that she was waiting to receive me in the room whose bright windows I was passing and repassing mechanically – a feeling I had never had before.

I do not know how long I walked up and down that evening; but as I strode I became gradually aware of a rising crescendo of noise from the direction of the town. There was a good deal of shouting, and I could see kerosene lamps moving hurriedly toward one focal point. Glad to have some form of distraction, I slipped on some clothes and ran toward the commotion. The excited crowd was just then moving off in the wake of a man who was shouting and gesticulating as if he had just been accosted by the Devil himself. I gathered from someone in the crowd that the man leading us had reported seeing a white man emptying a gun into a screaming white woman in a building a little further down the road, and had come to summon help. My blood raced madly; I elbowed my way quickly to the front of the jostling crowd and caught up with the man who was shuffling along, letting forth a stream of incoherent Hausa in which the words 'white man', 'fire', and 'smoke' kept recurring. I distinctly caught a faint scent of local gin, but I never stopped to question the man at all; and it was only when he turned into the 'auditorium' of Lokko's brand-new open-air cinema that I had the sense to stop short. It finally emerged that our friend had staggered into the empty enclosure and fallen into a drunken sleep in one of the seats that afternoon, and had opened his eyes several hours later just in time to see the villain of a blood-and-thunder thriller doing the heroine in in the approved manner. In no condition to stop and look twice at

107

what he saw, he had run out of the compound and down the street screaming for help. . . .

I did not wait to hear what the crowd would have to say to him. For me the whole ludicrous incident had been timely and salutary. It seemed in a flash to place in clearer perspective the incongruous situation in which I and my countrymen found ourselves. I could afford, if not exactly to smile at this unexpected interruption, at any rate to relax somewhat from the overwrought state I had been in previously. More important than the proof the incident had furnished that the gin of Africa will not mix with the bilge of Hollywood, it had jolted me to my senses by revealing starkly to me the ugly intensity which my own animosity could develop in an instant, and without the slightest justification. I felt now ashamed and disgusted with myself at being such a helpless victim of my own emotions – I who had prided myself that one of the marks of a good education was the capacity for acting calmly and reasonably at all times. I fell asleep after swallowing a stiff whisky and soda, chastened and mortified.

My head was very clear when I woke next morning. It was a Saturday, and I knew exactly what I wanted to do. The day was spent at my writing desk – drafting a letter to Samuel, carefully putting certain proposals to him. For overnight I had come to the big decision of my life – to devote all my energies to politics, so that first in Songhai and then later, I hoped, throughout Africa, I could help free men from domination by peoples of other races. I had narrowly escaped, the previous night, developing into a violently destructive racialist, with a soul poisoned by hatred. Instead, with a drunkard's help, I had found a better way of fulfilling what now I saw clearly as my destiny. I would work constructively with and for my people, instead of destructively against another. I would seek to give every black child within my reach the chance to prove himself, in favourable circumstances, no whit inferior in ability to his counterparts of different pigmentation. As the day wore on, my sense of vocation for and dedication to this task grew in intensity until it seemed to suffuse my whole being, and fill the very room I was in. I was only dimly aware then of what might be meant when I thought of 'every black child within my reach'. The extent to which I might be called to work for my fellow Africans outside Songhai was not clear to me at that time. I sensed all at once the meaninglessness of colonial boundaries in Africa; and realised that in the crusade upon which I was now embarking they would have to be treated as the doodlings of Europeans. But my immediate concern was not so much with the ultimate scope of the sacred mission placed in my hands, but with the nature of the first steps I must take in it.

It will be understood that what I was now doing was a complete *volte-face* in my personal habits, in my code of behaviour, even in my ethical and cultural standards. I could no longer be content with doing as much of what gave me pleasure as I could, and as little of what caused me discomfort or boredom. In a way I was experiencing a profound spiritual conversion. The life before me now was one of self-negation and self-sacrifice. I would have to give up many things which, innocent in themselves, might yet hinder the cause which was to become the purpose of living for me. I would have deliberately to judge my every action and decision by an invariable standard: will it bring me any nearer to my goal? In my dress, speech, and habits, I would have to proclaim my gospel, even though this might mean doing things in a way I might find inconvenient, and even distasteful. The biggest sacrifice I now found myself called upon to make was the exchanging of the licence of Christianity as taught us by the West for the discipline of Islam as brought us from the East. My conflict was intense, but brief; and when it was finally resolved I knew it could never be re-opened.

My pen travelled quickly and easily over the notepaper. I asked Samuel to consider urgently the possibility of returning to help me found a new political party. I explained to him that I was asking him, not merely because he was a Sagresan and I a Northerner (and our partnership consequently politically significant), but equally because he was my oldest and most trusted friend. I referred also to my great admiration for his inventiveness and lively imagination, all of which I said I thought would be important assets in planning and pursuing a political campaign such as I had in mind.

I went to see my parents that evening and asked them to help me choose a wife in the village. I had no doubt the request would come as a great surprise to them; for I was probably the first 'been-to' (that is to say, foreign-educated African) who was thus deliberately turning his back on the usual custom in this matter. 'Been-tos' normally married either foreigners or other 'been-tos'. But I now wanted to make a complete break, in my personal way of life, with Western habits and customs. It was not that I believed the African alternative to be, in every case, intrinsically the better; and certainly not that I derived more pleasure from adopting it. But I accepted that, in my new rôle of politician, the whole of my success would depend on knowing what gestures had to be made, and at what time.

The rest of the day I spent in writing out cheques and letters, to take out subscriptions to a representative selection of daily papers and periodicals published in or about Africa – the essential grist to the politician's mill. I posted my letters; then, while waiting for all this activity to bear fruit, I spent every spare moment I had from school during the following weeks travelling as far afield as possible in my car, getting to know people and places. I deliberately chose to wear African gowns on these journeys, and to speak English only when it was unavoidable, but I did not disclose to anyone the new sense of purpose in life I had acquired. I drew curious looks from friends and acquaintances, to be sure. 'Been-tos' in Lokko, like those in Sagresa, regarded the fancy-dress ball as the only suitable occasion on which to be seen in African dress. In all this I wanted to time my change of personal habits to take place well in advance of my overt pursuit of a political career.

The reply from Samuel brought me the utmost satisfaction. He took up my proposal eagerly, and said that it was, in a way, an answer to a prayer that had been more and more often on his lips in recent months. As soon as he could scrape together his fare, he would join me. My plans were taking shape.

For my parents had also been only too glad to meet my wishes and had promised to attend the next Dopo graduation ceremony on my behalf. They would then open negotiations with the family of the girl chosen as soon as possible, and make all the necessary arrangements for the marriage ceremonies.

The days now began to fly past. I sent Samuel his fare, and studied carefully all the periodicals which now began to arrive, making and filing many cuttings which I judged of interest or importance to the work we had ahead of us. My touring took me further and further away from Lokko, and I made a special point of making myself known to the chiefs and their elders everywhere I went. At the same time I was careful not to neglect my work as a teacher, for I knew that for some time to come my livelihood would depend on it. In fact it would have ruined my chances of success as a politician if it appeared that I had turned to that career merely because I had failed as a teacher.

I went down to Sagresa to meet Samuel's plane. A word in the ear (and a pound in the palm) of a *Daily News* reporter I knew resulted in a photograph in that paper two days later of me embracing Samuel like a long-lost friend outside the terminal. A caption underneath reported that 'rumour has it' that the two friends concerned were planning to found a new political party in the near future with the slogan: 'UNITY NOW; SELF-GOVERNMENT IN FIVE YEARS.'

The great mission on which my friend and I were now engaged may be thought to have had a somewhat unimpressive public launching. A newspaper photograph, a slogan, and then silence for several weeks hardly appear the best way of beginning a political career. But in fact some instinct had led us right from the start to the secret of capturing the political imagination of the African electorate at this time: a slogan, more arresting than practicable; and the creation of an atmosphere of mystery and secrecy which would encourage conjecture and speculation. Neither of us believed for one moment that in five years' time a Songhaian would in fact be attending a Commonwealth Prime Ministers' Conference. All we aimed at doing at this initial stage of our crusade was to start people talking about us.

But there was an unexpected and highly satisfactory result of the publication. The majority of people who saw it merely talked curiously about it. The older generation muttered darkly about the impetuousness of youth; but eight young men, five of them from the North and the others from Sagresa and the coast, came to see us during the course of the following week at my bungalow in Lokko, to inquire about the 'new party'. Lack of faith, perhaps, had prevented me from realising that there must be many Songhaians of an age and an education similar to Samuel's and mine who would respond immediately to such a call. Some of our later supporters might have been motivated by the desire to acquire personal power and fat incomes in ministerial office; indeed we were to learn deliberately to make use of many not altogether worthy, but politically useful, motives to swell our membership lists. But these early adherents, reacting immediately and with so little prompting to a call which at that time must have seemed so remote from reality – these were our true fellow-spirits.

For a month the ten of us met in my bungalow practically every day, working out our initial plan of campaign. And it was at this time that I had occasion again to marvel at Samuel's genius for hitting on ideas which would 'work'. While I drafted documents – articles for the press, pamphlets, posters, manifestos – he did the work of an American sales promoter. From his fertile imagination came plan after plan to promote our cause. Each one we examined together carefully and at great length, knowing that we could do so without the slightest risk of offending Samuel by candour as to what we thought of his ideas. When we were not planning, we were touring; carrying much further afield the task I had already begun in a small way – to get to know and to be known by the people that mattered in as many different parts of Songhai as possible.

We were a very mixed bunch, the original ten of us, in temperament and in vocation. Three were civil servants, who were technically forbidden from taking an active part in politics, so had to proceed very cautiously for the present. Two others were young barristers; newly qualified, and earning a somewhat precarious living in a country where the saturation point of barristers had long since been reached. Of the remaining three, one was a free-lance journalist, another a teacher like myself, and the third a district council clerk. By Songhai standards, I suppose all of us would have been regarded as well-to-do; certainly finance was the least of our worries at this time. A savings bank account was opened for the party in my name, and each of us put at least ten per cent of his income into it every month. In addition, every now and then one or the other of us would succeed in picking up a windfall for the party account from sources which we thought it imprudent as well as unnecessary to discuss with each other. Windfalls and fortunes in Songhai nearly all had a common origin in those days – in the forbidden but well-trampled diamond fields. We exulted secretly in the thought that at least some of the most highly concentrated form of wealth in Songhai (indeed in the world) was being applied to what had come to be for us now the most precious of causes. It never even occurred to us to wonder whether we were transgressing any laws in so doing.

We helped each other in other ways too during this month of preparation. Each of us accepted the necessity of mastering at least two of the six major Songhai languages. We made practice political speeches in these languages to each other, standing on my newspaper-protected dining table, both as exercises in thinking and expressing ourselves clearly, and as exercises in mob oratory, the need for which we knew would arise sometime in the near future. But we had already agreed that our initial method of proselytising would be something quite different.

Samuel had read somewhere of the mass literacy techniques a learned philologist had developed, and he had immediately seen the possibilities for our cause of that scholar's celebrated maxim 'Each one teach one'. Where a methodical system of spreading a gospel while maintaining the pitch of its fervor was required, there was nothing to beat the idea of each member of a small, devoted group undertaking to bring in just one equally dedicated convert every month, who would then similarly undertake to bring another in monthly. Apostates and lapses there would bound to be, but if even only half of those won by this method remained faithful to us, we reckoned we could not fail.

At times the possibilities of this geometrical progession seemed almost overwhelmingly exciting, I remember. Our determination to make this thing work was boundless, and our faith in ourselves and our cause inspired our whole lives. At Samuel's suggestion, we prepared pyramid-shaped charts, so that the name of each new convert to the cause could be recorded under the name of the person who had brought him in, and we could spot defaulters at a glance. We had a heated argument one evening when laying out these charts as to whether one name – mine – should head one giant pyramid, or whether each of us in the original ten should head his own. It was determined not to prejudice beforehand the free choice of an official leader, which would have to be made by all the members of our movement at some later stage. So I resisted firmly the idea of being symbolised now as the apex of the whole organisation. We eventually affixed ten identical charts to the walls of my study: ten pyramids of neat geometrical proportions, with all the little square bricks of which they were built blank except the one forming the apex of each, which bore the name of one of us. The rest awaited our converts.

We in Africa learned a long time ago something the people of Europe are only now discovering: that the human mind has almost illimitable powers over the body that houses it. For example, we know – we don't merely believe, but *know* from personal experience – that it is possible for one person to bring sickness or death to another without recourse to physical or chemical means. Three steps, simple to describe but not necessarily easy to take, are required for this purpose: first to get your victim to believe that you have the power to harm him; secondly to get him to believe that you have the desire to harm him; thirdly to perform in his presence or to his knowledge some action (it does not matter much what) which will symbolise the placing of the curse on him. His own mind will do the rest.

Similarly with good as with evil. We believe that success in life is much more a matter of faith and will than of intelligence or industry. As our small group of ten stood back to look at our blank pyramids on the walls of my room on the evening we finished putting them up, the certainty of success gripped us with an intensity almost intolerable. It was a sensation that came to all of us simultaneously; a sense of exhilaration, almost of achievement already. It was as if it were now only a matter of time before our goal would be reached; as if we had already done the essential task of willing and believing in the fulfillment of our dreams, and that it was now left to some other agency to bring them to fruition.

CHAPTER NINE

ONE DAY soon after this, Samuel and Kai-Kai, one of our two barristers, came excitedly into my bungalow with a copy of the *Daily News*.

'This dear old rag could hardly be more helpful to us even if we held all the shares in it,' exclaimed Samuel, jabbing at the front page. There was a reproduction of the photograph of Samuel and myself published at the time of his arrival from the U.K.; above it appeared in bold type the question 'Where is the new party?' and below it a short paragraph reminding readers that it had been reported some time ago that the new party was going to aim at ' U N I T Y N O W ; S E L F - G O V E R N M E N T I N F I V E Y E A R S .' Then followed a surmise of the kind newspapers (and politicians) love. The *News* suggested that it was being freely rumoured that the two founders of the party, together with a handful of devoted adherents, had gone into the wilderness to acquire, by methods which were not specified, the spiritual powers necessary to make the new venture a success. It was clear that it was this latter part of the publication which was responsible for Samuel's present elation.

The political value of spreading reports of this kind did not, of course, escape me; and I felt a mounting satisfaction as I read the paragraph a second time. Then all of a sudden a thought struck me, and I looked at my friend suspiciously.

'I don't suppose you had anything to do with this, did you, Samuel?'

'What, me? In my state of health?' And he gave me the most pained of looks, behind which I fancy I detected the ghost of a twinkle. For the expression was one which Samuel, who had developed increasingly jocular spirits since his arrival, was in the habit of using when engaged in mock self-defence. However, try as we would, we could get no more out of him on the subject; though there was plenty of proof later that, contrived or not, publications of this sort prepared the ground for us in a way few other things could have done. A far larger proportion of literate Africans accept as gospel what they read in black and white than is the case in countries with longer histories of literacy. Without admitting it (or perhaps even realising it), the man who, having been taught to read, is able to find little else of interest to read than the local papers, never outgrows the belief that a report which has achieved the dignity of print has also achieved the sanctity of truth. And the belief could be communicated even to the illiterate. During some of our later electoral campaigns, illiterates were often to be seen paying their twopence for a precious copy of the party paper, tucking it under their arm, and going off in search of a literate friend. Having listened attentively to the reading of every word, the unlettered but now edified owner would tuck it back under his arm, and march off proudly with it. Carrying this badge of truth, he could now command all the respect given to the ancient bearer of the oracle.

Before the formal launching of the party, I had one important mission to fulfil. My parents had told me that the formalities in connection with my marriage were almost complete. They had reached agreement with my bride's family on the question of the dowry, and other matters, and had paid the cost of her Dopo training themselves. She was a girl whom at the time I knew only very slightly, considerably younger than myself, and of excellent looks, character and family connections, my parents assured me.

As I drove to my father's house one Friday evening, my heart felt more than usually light. No doubt to some the idea of entering into a marriage with someone who is hardly known to you, and who has been found for you by others, will seem the very opposite of liberating. Yet I felt as if I were travelling now toward a point where my spirit would be set free in a sense it had never been before. I felt an exhilarating sense of discovery and release. I suppose it was largely the thrill of a new adventure, the sense of anticipation produced by the prospect of acquiring a wife who I at that time believed would bestow on me rights and pleasures without either responsibilities or duties.

It must be quite impossible for the European mind to comprehend the mental state of the two parties to a typical marriage in African tribal society. In Europe, the tradition is that the union must, ideally, be one impelled by powerful sentiments of love in both parties, and purified by a concern for the interests ond welfare, not of oneself, but of the other. In the perfect European marriage (and that of African 'been-tos') the theme that each is sacrificing something for the other must be constantly harped upon, and the martyr's crown should always be discernible through the cloud of confetti. If later that crown is found to weigh a little too heavily on either or both parties, the divorce court will relieve them of its weight. But right from the start you are forbidden to believe that the act of marriage is an act of self-interest.

The customary African marriage, on the other hand, is accepted by all concerned as being just that. Away from the 'Westernised' cities, you marry the most attractive girl that can be found for you, and at such time as you believe that your own physical and material interests generally require it. There is little or no pretence of flooding the life of a fellow creature with the rapture of loving and being loved, with the blissful companionship of united souls, or the altruistic search for ways of bringing pleasure to the beloved. The reasons for seeking wives are admittedly selfish, not altruistic;

and the same considerations determine the number of them who will ultimately be acquired, and the timing of each fresh marriage contract. The whole union is on a different, and a less idealistic level.

This is why, of course, the African bridegroom of this type has to pay in material wealth far more for his wife than the European and Europeanised bridegroom; for, in purely economic terms, he is getting far better value. The first pays in cash only, so has to pay a stiff price. The second ideally pays for his wife partly in spiritual currency, by giving part of his soul to her.

And yet, I reflected as I turned into the familiar compound, the irony of it all was that, taking a European divorce as marking the failure of a European marriage, the European form of the institution had failed in a far more spectacular way than the African form. For even on the rare occasions when an African village wife returned, or was returned, to her family, it could not be said with the same dismal head-shakings that the institution itself had once again demonstrated its imperfections. No; there had merely been an error of judgment; a bad bargain had been struck, and the party which had failed to give satisfaction always, on such occasions, had the decency to refund whatever had been paid.

What I did not at this time have any means of guessing, however, was the far greater truth that a coldly calculated materialistic bargain may, under suitable conditions, provide excellent soil for the growth of the most profound affections between two parties. To love at first sight and then marry need not be any more certain of success than to marry at first sight and then love, judged empirically.

I dare not lift the veil that protects our tribal marriage customs and ceremonies from the eyes of outsiders. There is already too little in this world that is sacred; and what Fatmata and I were required to go through during the next week must remain so. I was deeply in debt by the time everything was over, but I was absolutely satisfied with my parents' choice. Fatmata was as black as satin, and as soft. She had the teeth and smile of a goddess. The Dopo tutors had done their job well: she was a completely efficient lover and mother. I brought her home with swelling pride, and began at once to save all I could spare toward the cost of acquiring my second wife. My anti-Western revolt was gaining momentum.

Now, however, the affairs of our newly born party had begun to require so much of my time and energies that the question of resigning my teaching appointment was exercising my mind constantly. It was the constant travelling we all did that was making it virtually impossible now for me to do efficiently the job I was being paid to do. We had divided the whole country into ten sectors, and each foundation member had assumed responsibility for visiting every chiefdom in one of these sectors during the course of the year. Our plan was to meet the tribal authorities and acquaint them with our plans, and to get to know the leaders in each community. Sagresa was classed, for our purposes, as one sector, and Samuel was the obvious choice to work there. But we recognised from the beginning that his task was bound to be more difficult than that of the rest of us elsewhere. It was the only sector in which organised political opposition was to be expected, and in which there were powerful vested interests which would consider themselves threatened by the developments we were seeking to bring about.

Samuel remained at the same time a kind of organising secretary, responsible for planning the over-all development of the party. At his suggestion, we postponed having a mass rally until we could be sure of sufficiently large numbers to make an impact. The first public rally of a new organisation is crucial to its success. If it is poorly attended, and seen from the start to be no more than struggling along, the chances of ultimate success are very slight. But if at the opening rally membership can be shown to be not only enthusiastic but already large, the sound instinct of the human animal to move politically in herds will at once begin to work for, instead of against, the organisers. For organisations, as for individuals, it is true that nothing succeeds like success. 'Don't launch small snowballs,' Samuel repeated constantly.

But in fact from the very start our membership grew steadily. For the first three months it doubled itself, as planned, each month; and it was only in the fourth month that we had our first defaulter, who was promptly expelled from the party. Each of us had his own way of proselytising, but we all found that the idea of shaking off political domination of the white man within a stated period had a powerful appeal even to the most ingenuous of our countrymen. It opened up prospects (some of them admittedly false) of wealth more evenly shared, good jobs more freely available to the African, and all kinds of other undreamed-of rewards. In compound and hut and market place, we drew together our little groups of carefully selected listeners. We did not try at this stage necessarily to make of all of them members of the party, but merely to spread abroad knowledge of its existence and its aims, and to attract the interest and sympathies of as many of the 'big men' in each chiefdom as possible. When we decided the time was ripe to hold our first mass rally and throw membership open, we believed that we would reap a rich harvest.

My sector, or 'beat' as I sometimes affectionately thought of it, contained perhaps forty towns and villages, and was based on Lokko. Two fine new bridges had replaced the ferries which used to bottleneck traffic on the main road through the area when I was a schoolboy, and bustling townships had sprung up almost overnight around these bridges. Somehow I regretted the passing of those ferries, which used to oblige the proud motorist to squat cheek by jowl with the humble pedestrian a few inches above the muddy swirling waters, bound together in a fellowship of silent anxiety. The ferries were chained bow and stern to pulleys running along a stout wire cable which spanned the river a little way upstream from the actual line of crossing. The angle of the craft to the flow of water could be adjusted by shortening one or other of the chains, so that the pressure of the current drove the whole contraption apparently miraculously across in either direction. I had been fascinated as a boy by this, and by the great wealth of characters and languages to be found gathered on the ferry at all times of day.

Now, however, we flew high over the rivers on graceful, ruthlessly efficient bridges, as though we were deliberately being shielded from the temptation to look for diamonds in the glistening gravel below. One of these towns, Mabonta, became then, and has always remained, one of my favourite beauty spots. I found in its neat, park-like reservations a tranquillity and peace so profound that I sometimes wondered whether, had I found myself originally teaching in a spot such as this, I should ever have undertaken the life work I had now set myself to do. Such thoughts also came to me when, as so often, I sat with hundreds of others in a hollow square late into the night, dancing by the silver light of the ubiquitous pressure paraffin lamp. The throb of the drums, the clap of the hands, the shuffle of the feet, the lilt of the voices; hips swaying, nippled breasts bouncing, sweat streaming; happiness, I would think, happiness, the whole purpose of living, haven't these people got it already? Could they possibly be any happier or any more contented? Is it really in my power, in anyone's power, to improve their lot? Then I would look around for the sufferers from rickets or beri-beri or malnutrition, seldom absent from a company like that; and I would remind myself that, as the bodies of the few were wasted by disease, so the minds of the many around me were undeveloped, and cut off from access to a rich heritage of human thought and achievement. If they were happy, they

E

were happy by default; it was the happiness of the ignorant, the smile of the baby in sleep. And beyond them I saw other more sinister things, things which did not bear thinking about again, but which I knew were taking place on this very continent of Africa, and which I felt called to put right. And I would find relief for my feelings by joining the dancers in the centre of the square, and abandoning myself to the excitement of the dance. Starting in sedate and graceful fashion, it would mount in intensity and feverishness over a period of perhaps thirty or forty minutes, catching everyone up in its pulsating emotion. Men dancing, women dancing, each to himself or herself, oblivious, to all appearances, of all others; until at last the climax of the dance was reached, and the exquisitely controlled crescendo and accelerando reached their peak in a kind of frenzied, convulsed musical orgasm, which would leave everyone limp and sweaty, like a wet sock.

What pleasure did we find in dancing like this? It was, like all forms of art, a form of escapism through self-expression; of letting yourself, or part of yourself, go. Was the excitement which accompanied it martial or sexual in origin? I never stopped to ask. Was it moral, amoral, or immoral? I did not really care. The point for me at this stage was that I was rediscovering the African in me, a part of my nature which had been swamped and submerged during the last few years. And the discovery that I could still lose myself ecstatically in an art form so uncompromisingly African brought me now very great satisfaction.

Samuel's 'beat' included Bonfe, a small seaport to the east of Sagresa, and I would sometimes take a river journey down to it with him, as we all recognised that this would be a particularly difficult area to campaign in. It was the kind of place that seems to have a past without a future; where everywhere you turn you are reminded of what has been, but you look in vain for that ghostly thing newspapers refer to as 'the shape of things to come'. To get to Bonfe we would take a good motor road which led us across one of the few remaining ferries and on to a launch terminal further down the river, at Matro Jung. From here the way lay entirely over water; chugging lazily down the river Jung, past great red cliffs which seemed about to slide into the current; past the hardly less soaring green cliffs of forest, gloomy, but alive with sound and movement. The thick bush, the tall trees, the slender swaying bamboo would gradually give way to open country – as we neared the sea – to rice fields and mangrove swamps. You almost breathed a sigh of relief to see that man could here wrest some kind of livelihood from the soil without having first to undergo the labour of burning and clearing that matted undergrowth. Planting and weeding rice in swamps might be back-breaking; but at least it could be done without first destroying by fire every living thing on the site.

Instinctively, one looked for crocodiles in the muddy water; but if it contained any, we never saw them, and my idea of what they look like still derives from Whipsnade. Now and then, however, a scuffle of monkeys would set a-trembling the foliage of a mango or plum tree; and their chatter, high-pitched and lunatic-sounding, would bring jokes and rich, African laughter to the lips of the occupants of the little launch. Palm birds stood restless watch over their nests which depended precariously from the branches of the tree whose name they bore. They seemed to be quite used to the noise and smell of the boat's engine, and hardly took any notice of us. Many other gaudily plumaged birds would rise protesting, however, as we rounded a bend of the river, and take refuge further away from the banks.

Gradually, almost imperceptibly, the banks would retreat from us as we neared the sea; and the pilot would have to pay more attention to his landmarks and his bearings and less to the gossip and songs of his passengers. For songs there always were in plenty, rendered to the accompaniment of all kinds of instruments, native and foreign, and on all kinds of topics. The communal meals which first one group and then another on board had been having would cease; there would be a regular procession of passengers to relieve themselves over the stern; and all eyes would strain for'ard in the gathering dusk. We would thread our way amongst the host of small islands off that creek-cracked coast. Then finally, rounding the edge of the last small island, we would come upon Bonfe's tired, yellowing lights, beckoning mournfully to us from across the water.

Here, next morning, behind the long waterfront from which projected disused jetty after jetty, and on which stood buildings clearly larger than anyone had any present use for, we would sit in the homes of the men we believed mattered in that odd little community – the local councillors, the ministers of religion, the teachers, the government and commercial clerks. We would tell them quietly what we were trying to do, and would carefully make all those little gestures which we hoped would impress them with our sincerity. We always paid a visit to the old, crumbling cemetery, and displayed as much interest and knowledge as we could over the occupants of the graves. Here Samuel had a great advantage over me, for a large Sagresan colony lived here. He would often attract to himself a look of warm affection from a brave citizen by a knowledgeable remark about a name on a leaning tombstone. Then back we would walk through the grass-verged' paths which served perfectly adequately as streets, through the numerous groves of fruit trees, back to the small shuttered sitting-rooms where we drained a final gourd of palm-wine, and took our leave.

It was soon after one such visit that I decided that the time had come when I ought to resign my teaching appointment, in fairness both to my employers and to the party. We were gradually building up our party funds; for with a membership which was almost doubling itself every month the party was now well able to support Samuel and myself. My full-time energies could now be devoted to the increasingly demanding task of disciplining members who defaulted in the vital obligation of monthly recruiting. As we filled in a lower, longer row in each of our ten pyramids month after month, we left, inevitably, an increasing number of blanks, where defaults had occurred. We decided that we would relax our rules sufficiently to enable expelled defaulters to be re-admitted after a year outside the party. For our hopes were being realised to a degree I think few of us could have foreseen at the beginning; and we felt we could afford, now that the critical initial period was safely past, to temper the wind a little. The fear of suspension for a year, we hoped, would continue to give to our weaker brethren an incentive for winning their converts; whilst the prospect of readmission would prevent those who had fallen by the wayside from joining any other political organisation.

So we approached the first anniversary of our party with buoyant optimism. We had chosen as its birthday the day when our ten blank pyramids were finally attached to the walls of my room, and as this date came round again we began to make preparations for the public launching. Up till now the party had been in the nature of a purely private, exclusive organisation, admission to which was by introduction only. Now, however, that we had some twenty thousand names on our lists, we were confident that a mass rally to mark the opening of our membership to general subscription could not fail to succeed in clinching our success. It would also give us the opportunity of organising the party into branches, and decentralising to some extent its administration.

This time to contrive advance press publicity was hardly necessary. As soon as it was known that we intended to hold such a rally, we had as many reporters from Sagresa to interview us in our central office in Lokko as we could have wished. It must be remembered that we had virtually no competition at this time as a political party. The only two other parties which operated with any degree of success in the country then were based on sectional or regional interests, and could not vie with us in our claim to represent the interests of Songhai as a whole. This was something entirely new for the territory; and now that I look back on it from this distance of time, it seems almost miraculous that no one had thought of doing before what we were now engaged in doing.

That first rally was an experience I have never forgotten. We had sent out to every nominal member a letter urging that, unless prevented by illness, he was expected to attend. We stressed that on the impression we made at this first rally by our sheer weight of numbers, might depend the whole of our future success; and that the five years in which we were to pledge ourselves publicly to achieve self-government for our country would date from the day of the rally.

The venue for the rally was the subject of much anxious consideration. Finally we decided that the capital, although more expensive from the point of view of travelling than a more central place inland, must be the official birthplace for a party whose whole interest and concern set out to be national. So we hired for a weekend a sports stadium which had been completed a few years before on the outskirts of the city. A large covered platform was erected in the centre of the extensive field so that a small handful of us there could be seen by as many thousands of persons as could stand or sit on the grass and in the stands.

Other matters which had to be settled beforehand were the proposals to be placed before the rally as to a name, a symbol, a slogan, and an anthem for the party. They proved surprisingly easy to decide upon amongst the ten of us. 'Party for Unity and Liberation' expressed our two chief aims very well, and gave us a pronounceable set of initials, 'P.U.L.' The symbol we decided on was a diamond, surrounded by the words 'Many faces, but one object' – the brainchild of the ever-resourceful Samuel. But the official slogan remained what a year before we had let it be known it would be: 'UNITY NOW; SELF-GOVERNMENT IN FIVE YEARS.'

On the day itself everything worked precisely according to plan. Our members turned up in as large numbers as we hoped. We proved to have been wise in hiring the sports stadium for the whole weekend, for those delegates without relatives or friends in Sagresa were able to sleep there under some sort of cover. The rally itself was to be held in two separate sessions, on the Saturday evening, and the Sunday evening. This was the coolest time of the day, and as we were in the dry season we had no need to worry about the possibility of rain. During the first session we ten 'disciples', as we inevitably came to be called, introduced ourselves to the members of the party, many of whom had seen all our names and photographs continuously for months without ever setting eyes on more than one or two of us. I became aware, not for the first time, but in the most convincing of ways, of the value of being able to speak fluently two Songhai languages; for I was able to do some of my own interpreting. But then I think we all surprised ourselves (and each other) by the effectiveness of our oratory. I do not think this was the result so much of such practising as we had done amongst ourselves as of the very deep sincerity of purpose which filled us at this time, and which must have communicated itself to our audience. Samuel used Sagresan, of course, as well as English; here he was right at home, amongst his own people, stirring to its depths the sluggish backwater of Sagresan public opinion. And he did it magnificently. We carefully avoided any semblance of personal abuse of the politicians then in power; for we had decided that our strategy was going to be from the very start to present a constructive programme.

Indeed there was very little in the record of the party then in power which we could genuinely have attacked. They had led the country very slowly, very cautiously, a very little way along the path toward self-government. When the British had said, 'Move along', they had done so; when the British had said, 'Mark time', they had been no less prompt in obeying. No one's feelings had been hurt, no one had suffered either materially or emotionally in the process; and a few people, amongst them the Ministers themselves, had gained quite a lot.

No; there was precious little to attack – except the snail's pace at which things were moving. But this could effectively be attacked through the argument that only a party which was truly national in its membership could achieve the speeding-up in economic and political development which we were advocating.

'Take the iron ore mines, for example!' Samuel was in fine form that first evening, with the slanting crimson rays of the setting sun making his complexion look strangely rust-coloured, and his shirt russet. 'They've finished moving a whole hill of almost solid iron ore by steamer down the river and to Europe. Now they're doing the same to another hill. The Company is making far more out of it than the country; and if we go on at the present pace, before we get self-government many more hills will have been removed from under our very noses in exchange for a few *thousands* a year in taxes and royalties, instead of our mining it ourselves and selling it for a few *millions*. You all see what I mean, don't you?'

'Yes, yes.' A nodding, credulous chorus. All of us on that platform knew, of course, that it was not quite as simple as all that; but for the time being it would do, it would serve its purpose. We had learned always to draw our audiences fully into the act with us, to wait for answers to our rhetorical questions, making sure that those questions were so framed that the majority present were bound to give the answer we desired. This was much safer than attempting to be explicit as to the comparative advantages to the country of state ownership of the mines on the one hand, and private ownership on the other. Precision in politics seldom pays.

The sun plopped almost startlingly quickly beneath the horizon, and the quick dusk began to settle. I looked all around me at the sea of faces. They reminded me of the Mothers' Union audiences I had so often had to address in Britain, for some faces wore a smile, some frowns, some were just plain vacant. In front of us, to the right, to the left, and behind us they stretched. Samuel, like all of us who had spoken that afternoon, was having to turn constantly from side to side, with the microphone held hot in his hand. His complexion had now resumed a more normal hue, as had the dark-green slopes of the hills which formed the background to the scene. Dotted all over those slopes were the government and college bungalows, like birds' nests on a cliff. I wondered vaguely and unreasonably whether there were any binoculars trained on us from behind any of those windows. Neat red acalypha bushes had been planted at regular intervals all round the perimeter of the stadium grounds, and as their leaves rapidly lost their colour in the deepening dusk, they seemed like stooks of corn on the edge of a field. My gaze returned to the foreground, and I caught sight of Fatmata, in the very front row, listening with shining eyes and rapt attention to Samuel's closing words. As he finished and the warm applause started, her eyes met mine, and we exchanged smiles. I thought how lovely she looked just now, and realised that I had grown to love her very deeply. Her appearance had altered considerably since our marriage. Then, she had been well filled out, plump, a perfect figure, the result of weeks of beauty culture before her wedding day. For few African males find hour-glass slimness in the female attractive. Now Fatmata had lost weight through plenty of honest hard work; and with it had lost bodily beauty. But she had acquired an expression of gentle contentment and calm which I found it most pleasing to contemplate. At her request, I had recently set afoot the negotiations which were to lead to my second wife, Kayinde, joining our little household. I now approached this step with distaste, both my conditioned reflexes and my mounting affection for Fatmata causing me to shrink from actual polygamy.

But certainly it was not my marital relationships which were foremost in my thoughts that first evening of the rally. There was far too much for all of us to do. Our 'Each-One-Teach-One' policy of recruitment, having served its purpose to glorious effect, was now abandoned; and membership was thrown open to all and sundry. The money poured in and the cards poured out that evening under the floodlights. Next day, at the second session (which was for members only), the crowd was quite as large as at the public meeting, extremely careful though we were to check the cards of all those passing through the turnstiles. One after another our proposals were carried unanimously: the party name, the symbol, the slogan. Unknown to us, Samuel had succeeded in obtaining an uncut diamond from somewhere. He brought the evening to a dramatic climax by producing this somewhat undistinguished-looking object in full view of the excited crowd.

'Once,' he shouted defiantly, 'a diamond twice, three times the size of this one was found in this country. It was then the fourth largest diamond ever found anywhere in the world. Once cut and polished, it was worth thousands of pounds. But did it realise that much for us, the people to whom it belonged? Did it, I ask you?'

'NO!' yelled the crowd.

'No!' echoed Samuel. 'It did not. All those thousands of

red pound notes went into the pockets of white men, people who were not Songhaians, who were not even *Africans*. Thousands of pounds, which might have helped to build another fine college like the one you see over there, or a hospital, or bridges, or roads for our people. And why were others able to rob us like this? Because we are not united, and until we are we can never be free to manage our own affairs and control our own wealth. Our wealth and prosperity and happiness all lie in this diamond; let us be like it in having many faces united in one object. That's the message this stone has for us. Can anyone here think of a better symbol, or a more fitting slogan, for our new party than the ones we have brought before you?'

'NO!'

No indeed. For that diamond was to bring us, in an oblique way, more good fortune than we could foresee at the time. Samuel had forgotten (or had chosen deliberately to ignore) the law which at that time made the possession without licence of uncut diamonds illegal. He had forgotten too that the police were, at our request, in attendance at the rally. As he stood on that platform in full view of the thousands in the sports stadium holding aloft our newly appointed party symbol, a conscientious police sergeant sitting behind a microphone in a patrol car just inside the gates saw a rare opportunity to win promotion.

Samuel rounded off his speech with a carefully rehearsed scene, in which he counted publicly the last few seconds running out before six p.m. – which hour we had agreed was to mark the precise start of the five-year period in which we were pledged to obtain self-government. Whilst he was staging this melodramatic but completely successful act, the information room at police headquarters a few miles across town was thrown into a flap by an embarrassing radio report. What was to be done? Here was someone publicly breaking the law, and in full view of a large number of police officers.

Were they to be told to pretend they had not seen anything? How could they, when next day the papers would no doubt contain full reports, complete with photographs, of the illegal act? On the other hand what would happen if an attempt were made to arrest or detain the offender in front of a crowd so clearly in sympathy with him and his party?

So in the event nothing was done by the police that evening; and at a dance in the Community Centre later we celebrated in jovial mood the success of our venture. A crowded, hot affair this was, whose main value, I believe, was in giving a certain social tone to our party in the Sagresa community, and in raising a handsome sum of money for party funds. Sitting in the cramped, unsafe-looking gallery at the back of the hall (I didn't feel in the mood for much dancing), I realised suddenly that it was not merely wishful thinking to regard the scene below me as symptomatic of the new spirit we were awakening in Songhai. Here were Sagresans and Northerners swaying happily together on the dance floor, for the instant oblivious of the differences that separated them, and very much conscious of an immediate common interest. A modern dance band provided the bulk of the music for dancing, but at intervals would give way to a traditional band, the dancing to whose music was no less vivacious or popular. Makeshift party banners bearing our slogan already hung everywhere, and the party colour – pillar-box red – drove away the traditional gloom of the ancient hall. I sipped my whisky-and-soda contentedly, and, through the haze of tobacco smoke, saw my dearest dreams taking slow shape. . . .

CHAPTER TEN

THE NEXT DAY the police struck. A calvalcade of cars and lorries was streaming out of Sagresa, conveying delegates returning home from the rally. Samuel was coming to Lokko for a short rest, and at the Sagresa boundary we were stopped, and the faces of the occupants of each car scrutinised by officers. We learned later that the police orders were that on no account was a disturbance to be provoked, and so an arrest was to be delayed until Samuel was not surrounded by a large crowd of party followers. The authorities had accurately gauged the popularity and strength of our movement. They had hoped that the car in which Samuel was travelling might be on its own at the boundary, and that it might be possible to take him into custody quietly. But the procession of vehicles was still very much together at this point; and the officer in charge dared do no more than note the number of the car concerned, and then allow us all to pass unrestrained.

Thus it was only when we were approaching the outskirts of Lokko that the warrant was produced; and, with no one to witness it except Fatmata and myself (who were in the same car), my friend was taken off. We followed the police car helplessly to the station, where we heard a completely dumbfounded Samuel charged with being in illegal possession of an uncut diamond.

I had never before regarded impulsiveness as a trait of my wife's character. Fatmata had always appeared to me placid, almost phlegmatic in disposition, and certainly slow to wrath. I had never once seen her lose her temper, or even her patience, with anyone in our household. So it was with utter astonishment that I saw her, as the station sergeant completed the reading of the charge, fly suddenly at his throat and started pummelling him with all her strength on head and body, at the same time cursing in the most immoderate terms his parents, grandparents, and all his ancestors. Having been at last dragged away and calmed, Fatmata was in turn duly made to listen, quite uncomprehending, whilst a charge of assaulting a policeman was read to her. Following which developments no arguments of mine could persuade the ruffled officers to allow the two offenders to leave the station that night.

This first brush with the powers that be was to prove yet another blessing in disguise. But for the moment it upset me considerably. It appeared to be our first real setback. So far everything had been almost unbelievably plain sailing. This was the first time anything had gone wrong, and that night, after the numerous sympathisers had left, I felt suddenly lonely and tired. I had listened to many hot-headed proposals for forcing the authorities to release their prisoners; but I hardly realised that even as I lay in bed sleeplessly the news of their arrest was spreading far and wide throughout the country, creating, to our credit, a vast fund of hostile feeling against those who held Samuel and Fatmata

And yet I could not conquer my depression. For my determination that we should achieve our final objective without the use of force or violence in any form, and with due regard for law and authority, was as strong as ever; and I could not but regard this early falling foul of the law as a bad omen. I knew something of the forces ultimately at the disposal of colonial powers; I had heard and read how they had been deployed, and with what ghastly effect, during political riots elsewhere. I believed that the use of violence, and the flouting of authority, were boomerangs which usually recoiled painfully back on their senders.

When I called at the police station early next morning, it

was to find that the two accused had been separated. Samuel had been sent back to Sagresa – the 'scene of his offence', said the sergeant – whilst Fatmata was to appear that morning in a court in Lokko. Evidently the police were still very much on the alert to prevent the development of any disturbances as a result of the arrests. Now that the rally was over, Sagresa was a far safer place than Lokko in which to hold prisoner a leader of our party. Fatmata could be fined and released before too many of our supporters had heard of her arrest, or had time to travel into the village.

The sergeant who had been the object of my wife's furious attentions had had time to recover his equanimity by now, and he was without too much difficulty persuaded to allow me to take Kai-Kai in to see Fatmata in her cell before her appearance in court. I stated that Kai-Kai would represent her in court, though in fact I had no intention of doing any more than to ask his advice before the hearing. I did not want a prolonged case made of this, and felt that the best thing would be to comply with the evident wish of the police that everything should be concluded as quickly and with as little fuss as possible.

As soon as we entered the detention room, however, I saw that we were going to have a difficult time persuading Fatmata of the wisdom of this course. To my surprise, I found that she had realised instinctively the political benefits to be derived from what had happened. She wanted not only to fight the thing out, she said, but to make so much noise in doing so that the tribes would gather from every village where we had followers. Usually the most unquestioning and accommodating of wives, she now refused with a stubbornness which was quite astonishing to do as I ordered. The utmost we could get from her was a promise that she would assault no one else; but pleading guilty she said she would never do, arguing with shattering logic that the term 'pleading guilty' implied not merely that she had struck the officer (which she admitted), but also that she had done something wrong (which she hotly denied). And, she added, if anyone in court made such an implication about her she would express her feelings on the matter very clearly indeed.

For fifteen minutes I pleaded and remonstrated with Fatmata, for the first time in our married life. But she seemed to be enjoying the unaccustomed deference she was now receiving from me, and looking forward to its continuing. She asked me to ensure, if she were to be jailed for a period now, that arrangements for my marriage to Kayinde, already well advanced, would be speeded; so that I might not be left for long without someone to look after my home. As soon as my second wife had moved in, I was to be sure, she asked, to bring her to the jail to receive full instructions as to how to run the compound.

I realised that the girl was in deadly earnest about this. She wanted to make a martyr of herself, quite deliberately and quite calmly. Drawing on depths of perception and self-will I had never even suspected her of possessing, she was going to follow a course of action which she was convinced would in some way benefit the party at her expense.

When the hearing of the charge against her opened a few hours later, I was still a little dazed from the shock of this new insight into my wife's character. Fatmata's behaviour in court soon made me snap out of the daze. She was just about as insulting and insolent to everyone who addressed her as she could possibly be. Fortunately for her, the magistrate (an Englishman) could not understand what she was saying, and the interpreter tempered considerably in translation the vitriol of her words. Even so, there was no mistaking her tone. To the original charge was promptly added one of contempt of court, and we all watched wordlessly as she was sentenced summarily to six months' imprisonment.

The effect of this unrehearsed melodrama was precisely what the principal actress in it had hoped. The newspapers were full of pictures and stories of the defiant victim of imperialist agents. More important, the news was spread by word of mouth along the lorry-routes and by talking drums along the bush-paths both more rapidly and far more extensively than by the press. Within a fortnight of the event, I doubt whether there could have been very many villages in the country which had not heard of the African woman who had fought a policeman, and then insulted to his face the white man judge – and in his own court too.

In the meanwhile Samuel had been remanded in custody in Sagresa, after a preliminary hearing at which he had pleaded not guilty. He sent a message to say that he too intended to exploit, in the interests of the party, the publicity value of the case. The diamond he had exhibited at the rally had been identified as the property of a British mining company, and he had now been charged with receiving as well. He was hoping that this would be a test case. He and Kai-Kai wanted to try the whole validity of laws granting to foreign companies concessions in minerals dug from soil which, according to native law and custom, could itself never be alienated.

To Samuel's case, as to Fatmata's, the newspapers gave very extensive publicity. Some of them, of course, branded them both as hot-heads who were striking their heads in vain against the brick wall of imperial authority. Others, however, painted them in the colours of national heroes, fighting a case which, if successful, could transform the whole economic future of the colony. I knew that both interpretations were in varying degrees misleading; and I found myself wishing, not for the first time, that we had a paper under our control through which we could seek to influence the reading public. The publicity we were receiving I recognised, of course, for what it was worth. But I still wished I could have stressed the importance of changing evil laws by constitutional and legal means – as Samuel was seeking to do

– as opposed to the use of force to which my wife's immaturity and impulsiveness had led her.

There was also perhaps another, unadmitted, reason in my mind for not welcoming all these developments with as much enthusiasm as did most other members of the party. It must be remembered that the choice of a party leader had not yet been made. We were still at the stage of trying to bring some kind of order and organisation into our very large and scattered membership. One of the decisions at the recent rally had been that party branches should be formed in each district during the month following the rally. Elections of branch officers and executive committees would then be held, and these would take over from our overworked headquarters at Lokko the responsibility for managing the affairs and ensuring the growth of the party in the districts. When all branches had been thus constituted, a convention was to be called at Lokko of delegates from all branches, who would elect from amongst themselves the national officers of the party; including, for the first time, its official leader.

I suppose even at this early stage I must have realised that Samuel's imprisonment would be bound to bring publicity and popularity to him personally, and I recognised the first stirrings of jealousy within me. Whatever the reason, the more I thought about the developing situation, the less I liked it.

I travelled down to Sagresa for the hearing of the case against my friend. The stately law courts on Prince Henry Street had recently been given a fresh coat of whitewash, and their walls gleamed in the bright morning sunlight as we pressed up the unnecessarily ornate stairway which ruined the appearance of the building's façade. There was a very large crowd waiting to hear the case, but places had been reserved for me and for others amongst our party leadership; and we were at once shown into comfortable seats in the well of the court. The air in the packed room was already foul.

Looking at the electric fan whirring away on the judge's bench, I wondered vaguely why his lordship should prefer breathing bad air which was on the move rather than bad air which was static, as the rest of us were doing.

Samuel's counsel were Kai-Kai and Konadu, the other barrister amongst our original ten. Their brief was very carefully prepared; and the argument delved deep into technicalities concerning the native system of land ownership in the protectorate, the possibility of alienating mineral rights there, and the rights and obligations of the tribal authorities in whom was vested perpetual title. I do not suppose more than a tiny fraction of those present in that court that hot morning could follow the arguments. But what became inceasingly clear to me as I strained every nerve to keep up with the verbal intricacies was that there were here two legal systems in head-on conflict. There was on the one hand the system of native law and custom, distilled from the social behaviour of countless generations of our people; and on the other, the Western system of enacted statute law, contained and defined in ordinances and other legal instruments. The judge no doubt saw the conflict too; and since native law is so much less brittle than the other, and may be broken, not less easily, but certainly less noticeably, he found it expedient to resolve the issue in favour of the imported code. And perhaps, technically speaking, he was absolutely right, and Samuel was absolutely wrong. It was just too bad that the law his lordship was trained and paid to interpret was the law of the land, without being the law of the people.

Samuel's sentence was two years' imprisonment; and many wept in open court as it was passed. There was no alternative of a fine, though that was what all of us in the party had hoped for. The crowd in court groaned a great, heavy groan as he was led back down the steps out of our view, and the judge rose at once with as much haste as was compatible with dignity.

Those two years were a period of continued rapid growth for our party. Much to my relief, there was no outbreak of violence, not even any disturbance of importance, as the news of Samuel's imprisonment spread. What did happen was the conversion to our cause of many thoughtful persons, to whom the extent to which our rights as Africans over our own property had been proscribed by laws of foreign origin had now been forcibly brought home. In prison Samuel re-received very many visitors; and, not for the first time, a colonial government in Africa discovered that imprisoning politicians for actions technically illegal but politically popular can defeat its own ends.

So the day when we must choose our national officers came nearer. I had been elected chairman of the Lokko branch, and Samuel, still in prison, was enthusiastically made chairman of the Sagresa branch. Each of the other eight foundation members had also secured a branch chairmanship. We at Lokko were to be hosts for the convention; and we spared neither trouble nor expense to make the occasion memorable. We had a brand-new barri constructed on a piece of open land, and the surrounding area was carefully laid out and decorated. It was planned that for a week we should hold a series of open meetings and functions, mainly with the intention of getting to know each other thoroughly. We hoped too thereby, as a sideline, to make a suitable impression on the good townsfolk of Lokko; and, through the press, on the people of Songhai generally. At the same time a small committee under my chairmanship worked late into each night at my bungalow drafting a party constitution for consideration at the convention. It was a well-chosen, well-balanced committee, of the type that really seems to be able to be getting somewhere the whole time it is working. There were three lawyers on it (including Kai-Kai and Konadu), an accountant, a teacher, and myself; and we had before us copies of the constitutions of numerous political parties both in Africa and abroad.

The last two days of the conference were held *in camera*. The first of these two days was taken up with the adoption of our draft constitution, and this went through with no difficulty at all. Our lawyers had succeeded very well, I think, in combining clarity with brevity, and had sought to provide for all the foreseeable organisational requirements of the party. We had decided that it was essential that the party organisation become fully democratic as quickly as practicable. We had therefore provided that while the first party leader should be elected by, and from amongst, the delegates then assembled, all future leaders should be elected by secret postal ballot of the whole party membership.

Late that evening the whole constitution was unanimously adopted, and our party became legally constituted for the first time. The following day we had to choose the party leader and his officers; and I have often wondered since whether the outcome of those first elections would not have been different had I not been in the chair at the meetings of the constitution-drafting committee. As chief exponent to the conference of the draft constitution, I had naturally attracted to myself most of the limelight. It was generally known, too, that the idea of founding this party had originated with me. But still Samuel, by becoming a prison undergraduate, had made his name just as widely known amongst the rank and file of the party members as was mine, and was universally regarded as the martyr of our cause.

I must confess that, right from the start, and consistently throughout until the election was over, I hoped anxiously, and entirely selfishly, that I might be chosen as first leader. With the selfishness there must have been self-conceit – the conviction that no one else would succeed in piloting the party's course as well as I. But in self-defence I must add that the fulfillment of my life's aim of demonstrating that the African was in no sense inferior to the European had now become the only thing that really mattered in this world. I felt sure that, given the chance, I could realise that aim. I could not be as sure of anyone else's single-mindedness in this matter as I was of my own, and I wanted to take no risks. Samuel had been, since our school days, the most loyal of friends; and indeed the certainty that he would remain faithful to me whatever the outcome of the elections bolstered my hopes, and nourished my pride.

As Conteh (the temporary organising secretary, who was in the chair at the election meeting) rose to declare the result of the secret ballot, I found myself trembling with excitement, and praying with passion. No one else in that cool barri, as I looked around nervously, appeared to be attaching quite as much importance to the election as I was. I suppose that the others knew that, whoever won, the party would not lose the services of any of the candidates. It had been agreed that the runner-up should be automatically appointed Deputy Leader, and to no one else there could the election have seemed the matter of life and death that it seemed to me.

'The result of the voting in the election for the post of first leader of the party is as follows' [Conteh's voice sounded to my taut senses almost bored]: 'Kamara, 212 votes; Cole, 163 votes; Kai-Kai . . .'

But I hardly heard any more. A sentence I had read some years before in a British periodical sprang unexpectedly into my mind. The writer had been dealing with the dilemma which the British rulers of Cyprus were facing at that time as a result of the demand of the majority of the islanders for *enosis*. He had concluded with a sentence which now burned in my consciousness with great clarity: 'And we (the British) must always remember that we are dealing with an intelligent, European people (the Cypriots) – not backward African natives.'

God had now given me the opportunity I needed to make

144

it impossible for any intelligent person to make a remark like that again.

Kai-Kai pushed a telegram into my hand. It was from Samuel in his cell in Sagresa. Addressed to Kai-Kai, who was asked to hand it to me if I were elected, it conveyed to me my best friend's heartiest congratulations, and his assurances of unwavering loyalty.

CHAPTER ELEVEN

K A Y I N D E   W A S   perhaps fifteen years younger than I, and
unlike Fatmata, could boast of a primary education. She had
a close-cropped head of hair which never seemed to grow.
A little on the thin side perhaps, she had nevertheless perfect posture and carriage, and to watch her walking across
the compound with a bucket of water or a basket of cassava
on her head was something from which I always derived much
pleasure. She had excellent dress sense, too. She would spend
a great deal of time at the sewing machine, turning out lap-
pas, smocks, headties, of every design and hue; and almost
as much time again in front of the mirror, working out new
ways of wearing and draping the garments. And the whole
time this was going on she would make me feel it was really
being done to please me. Without saying very much to me,
she would always take the trouble to walk slowly down my
line of vision as I rested on the veranda hammock or sat at
my desk looking out of the window. She was a most affec-
tionate young lady. Fatmata had warmed to me only very
gradually; Kayinde was prepared right from the start to
lavish on her husband her love, and to arouse his. I have often
reflected on the stubbornness with which the differences in
temperament of these two girls had survived the rubber-
stamping uniformity which Dopo attempts to impose on the
marital behaviour of its members.

Kayinde and I often went to see Fatmata during the first
few months of our marriage. She was not unhappy in prison,
and much more concerned about how Kayinde was managing the household and caring for me than about herself. The
junior wife would be given a long list of instructions as to

what to do and what not to do, and exhorted above all to make sure she bore me a son as soon as ever she could contrive this. I realised during these visits for the first time that Fatmata must be feeling keenly her failure up to the present to give me a child. She saw in Kayinde an opportunity to make sure that her husband would not remain for much longer in the humiliating position of being without a legal heir. A childless home is, elsewhere, no more than sad. In rural Africa it is often a positive disgrace.

The volume of work I had to do for the party, already considerable, now increased many times. The constitution of the territory provided for a general election before the end of the year, and all our energies were now devoted to winning that election and coming into power. We were going to leave nothing to chance, confident though we were of success; and electioneering was meticulously planned and carried out, chiefdom by chiefdom. We started our campaign in the week following my election as a leader. Although the local branches were given direct responsibility for selecting their candidates and deciding on detailed tactics, they drew heavily on headquarters for advice, literature, and funds. Then, too, the party manifesto had to be centrally prepared.

In this document we concentrated on making our claims realistic and practical rather than arresting. We still retained in our platform our cental plank of aiming at self-government within five years from the date of the party's foundation. It was indeed no longer necessary to make extravagant claims in order to win support; on the self-government dateline we retained only because we now genuinely believed it would be adhered to, should we be returned to power. And not one of us doubted but that we should be.

One of the decisions of our first convention had been that the leader of the party should be entitled to a salary from party funds at least equivalent to that he earned in the last professional appointment he held, and in any case not lower than £1,000 p.a. I now had no personal financial worries; and as a secretary had been appointed to help me with my work, I found I could give my undistracted attention to the broader problems of policy planning. Before really getting down to the task of supervising centrally the election campaign, I decided I must seek the quietness and shelter of a week's retreat in my parents' home.

Two reasons led me to this decision. In the first place, I was beginning to feel the reaction of fatigue following the tensions and excitements of the past few years. I had been working far harder during that period than I had ever done before, and with a one-mindedness more whole-hearted than I had lavished on any cause, the School Certificate Examination not excepted. Now that it seemed certain that the wherewithal for achieving my ambition was placed in my hands, I began to feel for the first time the strain of those late nights and hectic days, and the need for a complete break from their routine.

Secondly, I wanted time in which to think in an undisturbed atmosphere. There was a great deal to be pondered over, which required seclusion and freedom from the interruptions of the telephone and of callers. The precise wording of the party manifesto had to be decided. The content of the party programme had to be thought out – concrete programmes in all fields of national development – constitutional, social, and economic. I did not intend, therefore, to abandon work during this period; rather was I hoping to get a change of environment, and to think and scribble with my feet up, as it were.

I think also that the need to report to my parents in full the new direction into which my life was turning, and to ask their blessing on it and seek their advice for the future, must also have been presenting itself strongly to my mind at this time. I could move no further, I felt, without seeking the collective blessing of parents, uncles, and all available relatives.

The reporters all wanted to know where I was going. When I told them that my destination would have to remain 'undisclosed', I was not seeking further publicity through spreading a sense of mystery about my movements (though no doubt Samuel nodded approvingly when he read my reply). I was hoping, somewhat vainly, that I would be able to find in my parents' home respite from publicity as much as from my normal routine. But, as on the earlier occasion when Samuel and I had gone to earth, the speculations soon broke out again. My political enemies spread the word that my mother kept a pot full of magical ingredients continuously on the boil in my interest. My presence at the fireside from time to time was apparently necessary, though whether to taste the witch's brew, to stir the pot, or to fan the flames, no one seemed quite sure. And all this was invented for the benefit of the European and American news agencies, who lapped it up eagerly.

In fact, the evening of my arrival saw me seated in the family circle around a silver-bright lamp outside my father's hut, feeling much less important, and much less prominent, than before. I had saluted elaborately all my seniors. I was now telling my people what no doubt they already knew, but which, until they heard it from my own lips, they would profess not to know.

'Father.'

'Yes, son.'

'My party made me last week their leader. The leaders of the party came from all parts of the country, and after several days of thinking and talking they decided that I should lead them in trying to win the next elections. If we are successful, as I know Allah means us to be, I shall have to leave Lokko and go to Sagresa, to take charge of the whole government of Songhai.'

'It is good, my son. Allah has always made me believe that you would do well for your country and for your family and for yourself; and I thank him that he is now making this come true.'

I gave as much detail as I could remember of the circumstances in which this honour had been bestowed on me, and as much detail as I considered prudent as to our party plans for the future. The family listened attentively, and, on the whole, approvingly; and I was solemnly urged by one after the other of my elders never to grow so swollen with pride that I forgot or neglected the people from whom I had sprung.

As I looked at my parents, I suddenly realised how old they were. My father, once to me a heroic figure of strength and height, was now showing the strain on face and posture of years of hard, unremitting toil on the land and the river. The closing years of a man's life, like the closing minutes of the dying day, seem to run out much more quickly in Africa than in Europe. There are no disguises to wear on the face of old age; nor, if there were, would anyone wish to use them, and lose the respect which wrinkles and grey hairs earn their wearers. My father's hair was now quite white, his face wrinkled and wizened; and as he sat crouched in his chair, only his sharp little eyes seemed to be alive and moving. The white, hot light blanched still further the mass of short, crisp hair, and seemed to accentuate the lines of the forehead and cheeks. My mother carried her age much better. She had never put on any weight to speak of, but half a lifetime of child-bearing had sapped her strength, emptied her breast, and bowed her figure. She still carried on her petty trading, more out of habit than necessity. But she spoke rarely, and her smile was slow and sad. Only her face remained remarkable, the skin still smooth, the features regular and symmetrical, and the expression contented. These two, now at the head of our family (my grandparents and grand-uncles having all died) represented for me the highest wisest authority I recognised under God.

Under such a roof did I spend my week of rest. Most of it was passed in a hammock under the mango tree sleeping, reading, scribbling, or simply thinking quietly. There was only one break in this relaxed regimen. About halfway through the week, I received a note from the local District Commisisoner asking me to come and have a drink with him at sundown the following day. I was surprised at this invitation, as to the best of my belief I did not know the man, and had never expected for one moment to be thus honoured. However, seeing in it an opportunity to get to know yet another person of influence, I accepted it.

I drove up the winding laterite curve toward the block of office buildings in front of which they were just lowering the Union Jack; and then round behind the clock to the stilted bungalow where the D.C. lived.

Jim Anderson was now grey and stout, obviously nearing retiring age in the Service; and a little disappointed that in thirty years he had made so little progress in his chosen career that he was still only a District Commissioner, and that in one of the last of Her Majesty's colonies to attain self-government. However, jobs had become increasingly difficult to secure in the Colonial Service during the past few years. Jim Anderson was grateful for small mercies, and determined to make the best of them. He had not lost his sense of humour; he was, after all, he said, still a demigod in his district: local squire, magistrate, sheriff, chief constable, and everything else all in one. And if he had not attained to the full divinity of, let us say, a governorship, why, nor had any other D.C. for a long time now. It was a dying race of gods, that.

So he had invited me to drinks, not because he was in need of educated company (which he had long ago learned to do without), but merely, it seemed at first, to exchange reminiscences. He greeted me warmly, and the first few hours passed pleasantly enough. He seemed to have been kept in close touch even with my early career (by the now reconciled missionaries, I wondered?). Then abruptly his manner changed. He was back on Her Majesty's Service.

'I must congratulate you on your election to the leadership of the P.U.L., Mr Kamara. I thought your friend Samuel Cole, who is serving that unfortunate sentence in Freetown, might have given you a better run for your money than I hear he in fact did.'

(It's amazing, I thought, not for the first time, just how much these chaps get to hear of what goes on in the country.)

'Thanks for the congratulations,' I replied briefly, changing my mood to suit his.

He contemplated me uncertainly for a moment or two through blue wisps of cigarette smoke, while the golden bubbles followed each other silently up to the surface of our whisky-and-sodas.

Then suddenly, as if taking a plunge: 'I understand your party is promising self-government within five years,' he said.

'Do you consider us over-optimistic?' I felt it would be safer for me to ask questions than to answer them.

'A prospect you regard with enthusiasm I tend to view with dismay, you know. My bread and butter may depend on your not achieving self-government before I reach retiring age.' There was a twinkle of the old humour in the small grey eyes, but it was short-lived now.

'I don't think you need worry about that. We shall need the help of people like yourself for a very long time, whatever happens – or at least of those with technical jobs. And those with whose help we feel we can dispense, or who choose to leave us voluntarily, we shall make sure are suitably compensated.'

'I'll be quite candid with you, Mr Kamara.' He leaned forward, with one of his sudden, brusque gestures, so that the cane veranda chair creaked protestingly. 'I think, as do many others who are in a position to form a sound opinion, that you are going to arouse a lot of false hopes, and unsettle a lot of people both on your side of the colonial fence and on mine, if you go ahead seriously with this slogan about self-government within a stated period. Have you considered again recently, since your election, for example, whether it might not be wiser to make promises you can be sure of keeping?'

I said nothing for a few seconds. I was trying to decide whether this man was speaking on his own authority, or whether he was acting on instructions from somewhere further up the bureaucratic ladder which stretched between his humble bungalow and Government House. I decided the latter was probably the case.

'May I reply to one candid question by asking another?' I said.

'Please do.'

' "Sayest thou this thing of thyself . . . ?" ' I watched attentively his first reactions. But he made no effort to disguise them.

'Well, if you really want to know,' he said, raising his glass nonchalantly to his lips, 'His Excellency himself is interested.'

'Somehow I had a suspicion that that was the case.' I felt already that I could gain quite a lot, and lose nothing, by this evening's drinking session with Mr Anderson. 'Did His Excellency suggest you should give me that particular piece of advice?'

'No; that, at least, was done off my own bat. But H.E. has given a whole lifetime to the service of one part or another of our crumbling colonial empire; and he has become a pretty shrewd judge of what will help, and what hinder, the advancement of the people of a dependent territory. For what it is worth, you can take it from me that he is genuinely convinced that you will do more harm than good by attempting to confine an advance toward self-government within the framework of a timetable.'

A picture of the present occupier of Government House settled into focus in my mind's eye. The House itself was an ultra-modern glass and concrete eyrie erected somewhat incongruously on ancient foundations which had once supported a stout citadel. Sir Horace Montague-Bidborough was a small, birdlike man, with a beaked nose and gimlet-sharp eyes, who it was said kept to himself a great deal and spoke only when he could not escape it, but was a brilliant colonial administrator. I had set eyes on him only once, when he came to Lokko to preside at a local assembly of chiefs and to open some new buildings at the school. On that occasion I remember that under his ceremonial plumed helmet he had looked more birdlike than ever, rather like a ruffled cockatoo.

'I am flattered that His Excellency and you should have considered us worth advising,' I said. 'Please assure him that his views on the matter will be passed on to the party's executive committee.'

'Would you consider it impertinent of me to suggest that you use your influence on that committee to ensure at least a serious reconsideration of the matter along the lines I have suggested?'

I decided it might be prudent to bring the evening to an end as soon as possible. 'Frankly, I should,' I answered, draining my glass.

But Colonel Blimp is not so easily upset. There was only the briefest of glances in my direction, and then the apparently easy, self-assured air was resumed, and the conversation changed. A few minutes later, however, the black mosquito-boots crashed off their pouffe and onto the wooden floor with unmistakable firmness, and my host rose

'Have another whisky-and-soda, Mr. Kamara?'

This was my cue. 'No, thank you, I'd better be getting home. Got to give the old folks at home as much of my time as possible, you know. Thank you very much for the drinks – and the advice.'

'That's all right. Hope you won't live to regret not having taken it.'

Of course, I said to myself later, both H.E. and the D.C. are genuinely convinced that it would be harmful to Songhai to be hurried, as they would put it, toward self-government. They are not conscious of acting in their own interest, or in the interests of the country they represent. But in spite of (or perhaps because of) their life's work, they can never understand that freedom can be sweeter than orderliness or even prosperity; for they have themselves never been in bondage. After this, I never heard another word on the subject from any government official, and concluded that those then in authority had realised that we were not going to allow them to divert us from our pursuit of a policy we believed right.

But at least Anderson's way of doing things, although circuitous, was clean and above the belt. The Britishers who come out to the colonies in government service may be very race-conscious, but they are also carefully selected from among the ranks of the best educated – in the widest and best sense of the word. On the other hand, colonial politicians, like all politicians, have so often come to power by giving reign to precisely those urges and inclinations which people of good breeding the world over try to keep in check – the inclination to draw the derision and scorn of others upon one's rivals, for example; and the urge to acquire as much personal power and wealth as possible. Many of the members of the British Colonial Service represent not the average but the cream of their countrymen both in intelligence and in educational attainment. Unfortunately as the colonies advance toward self-government the African politicians with whom the British officials come into contact, and are inevitably compared, have usually been much less well prepared

F

for their careers than the latter. Politics is unfortunately still widely regarded as a profession something less than honourable in Africa, as I was now to discover afresh.

I cannot profess to have been entirely taken by surprise by the next attempt, from an entirely different direction, to turn me aside from my set purposes. The length to which the conspirators went in order to achieve their ends was somewhat unexpected, however.

A few weeks after getting back into harness at Lokko, I heard that a branch of the party which had recently been formed amongst the diamond mine workers in a remote village along the coast was having a good deal of difficulty in selecting officers, nominating a party candidate, and generally getting the branch organisation working. I decided that as this was a key branch with a large potential trade union membership I would pay the branch a visit myself to help straighten things out. The workers' vote was one which we had decided to spare no pains in securing.

I was not able to leave for the mines for a week or so after having decided on the trip, partly because I had an appointment to receive a delegation from the political party then in power in Songhai, the National Union of Colonials. This party, setting out, as its name announced, to unite in one cause all the people of the Colony, had soon lost its early enthusiasm, and lapsed into a well-paid, well-appointed, sleeping partner of British imperialism. Its leaders saw little need, now that they were enjoying official and unofficial fruits of office, to pursue their original objectives with any vigour.

Now, however, with our leaping membership figures published in every paper in the territory, the N.U.C. had been stung out of its complacency, and was, with something close to alarm, realising that its days were numbered unless it did something, and did it soon. Hence the delegation which passed through the archway of my compound one wet Saturday afternoon with a proposal a thousand times more shocking than anything Mr Anderson or H.E. could have said.

The chief spokesman of the delegation was a Mr Wright, a stout, bespectacled back-bencher in the House of Representatives, who began by assuring me that he spoke with the authority of the leader of the N.U.C. himself. His proposal which he entreated me to consider most carefuly (as he was sure, he said, that the whole future well-being of the people of Songhai hung upon my accepting it), was that the N.U.C. and the P.U.L. should merge.

'After all, we are all fighting for the same thing,' he declaimed pompously, watching me all the while a little too closely out of small, piggy eyes behind thick-lensed spectacles. 'We all want the best for this dear country of ours.'

'I do not doubt that for one moment,' I answered warily.

'Don't you think,' he went on, 'that we will conserve our energies and resources for the real enemy if we merge, instead of dissipating them by trying to cut each other's throats?' He looked round for support from his colleagues, and got it in the form of slow nods.

'That may depend on whether or not we agree as to who is "the real enemy". Perhaps it will help me and my party colleagues to come to a decision on your proposal, if you would state now what, or whom, you consider to be our real enemy,' I replied.

The eyes seemed to open wider for a moment and then narrow again behind the thick lenses.

'I should have thought the answer was pretty obvious,' he said softly, in between sips at his fourth glass of Drambuie and soda; which, not surprisingly, was inducing in him a series of violent belches. 'Ignorance, disease, wastefulness of talent and resources, undernourishment, poverty – these are our enemies, in Songhai, as everyone can see for himself.'

'And Imperialism?'

'Ah! Imperialism.' He drained his glass and gestured to my steward to give him the mixture as before.

'Yes. Would you say that that too must be fought, or not?'

My guest got some more wind off his chest, relapsed into a thoughtful silence for a few seconds, and then suddenly gestured to me to follow him out onto the veranda. I told the steward to fill up the glasses all round, and joined him, apologising to my other guests.

It occurred to me afterwards that it was perhaps the Drambuie that loosened Mr Wright's tongue to such an extent that he divulged to me what must certainly have been intended to remain top-secret within his party counsels. Or perhaps he genuinely believed that, by taking me so completely into his confidence, he woud be able to persuade me to accept his proposal for a merger. Whatever the case, what I now heard came as a stunning surprise to me.

We leaned over my veranda rail, looking at the rain belabouring the somewhat anaemic zinnias which since Fatmata's absence had fought a losing battle in our garden against the combined forces of poor soil occasionally moistened by soapy bath water and excavated by scratching hens. Here I learned that, following the cession of Simonstown to the Republic of South Africa, the United Kingdom and Songhai governments had agreed that it was to their mutual interest to develop Sagresa into a major naval base. It was a neat little scheme. All hope of the territory ever achieving self-government was to be abandoned. Instead, a comprehensive ten-year development plan was to be drafted, towards the financing of which the U.K. government would contribute a considerable sum of money. In return the U.K. would be allowed to build an extensive naval base and two large air bases in the territory and to hold indefinite leases in these. The possibility of associating the territory more closely with the United Kingdom legislatively and administratively would then be considered; but it was made quite clear that all advance towards independence was to cease forthwith in Songhai.

'So you see,' my informant concluded with an expansive gesture of his stubby arms, 'to pursue self-government now as you people wish to do is crying for the moon. The British will never grant it; nor do I honestly think it is in anyone's interests that they should, things having turned out as they have.' A thought suddenly struck him. 'Of course, you'll understand that I have told you this in the strictest confidence, and purely out of a sense of patriotism.'

I was too taken aback by his revelations even to answer him for the moment. I was gazng into space, turning over in my mind the incredible bargain struck between my own country and the British. Although Mr Wright had not mentioned it, I could see at once that the N.U.C. was certainly not going to be the loser if this sordid bargain went through. A freezing of the constitutional *status quo* in Songhai was entirely to the advantage of the party in power. Our franchise was still very far from being democratic, still retaining an exclusive property qualification. The electorate was therefore less responsive to changes in public opinion, and more inclined to conservatism, than it would have been under a sysytem of universal suffrage. Moreover, this agreement once concluded, the representatives of British authority in Songhai, from the Governor down to the humblest Assistant D.C., would regard it as their duty to keep in power the political party which had given to Her Majesty's Forces such invaluable assets. And there were still thousands of little ways in which the D.C.s particularly could influence the results of both local and general elections in their districts.

Mr Wright's party bosses had seen in the rise of our own party, just at the time when they were thus entrenching their own position in office, a most unwelcome threat; and were seeking to eliminate it by this proposal of a merger. If we were prepared to give up our aim of leading Songhai toward complete autonomy, then we could share with them the expectation of an indefinite tenure of political office, supported powerfully by the mosquito-booted agents of Pax Britannica. They could have chosen no more convincing way of bringing home to me the extent to which greed for political power and influence had come to replace patriotism as the driving force behind their present careers.

I realised suddenly that my visitor was still waiting for my answer. I still did not know in precisely what terms to express to him my feelings. Misinterpreting my hesitation, he said, 'There's no need to say plain yes or no now, you know. Why not go and think it over, and discuss it all with your friends – all, that is, except the confidential bit I told you about? In any case, I am feeling in need of a siesta just at the moment, if you don't mind. Let me know first thing tomorrow.'

He ambled off into the living-room; and, with the rest of his delegation, was soon climbing into the car which was to take them back to their hotel.

The next day, I was able to tell a somewhat more receptive Mr Wright quite clearly, and with as much force as I could muster, that I would not even consider putting such a proposal before our party; and to explain to him why. He seemed only mildly surprised, for I think that he was an astute man. It was probably long association with politicians whose politics had lost all their morals and whose minds all their agility that had made him see any possibility of success in a mission of this sort.

There were, however, minds both more agile and more evil than his at work. I was free now to leave Lokko to visit our ailing branch. I travelled to Sagresa first by road, as there were one or two friends (including Samuel) I wished to look up there; and then proceeded by launch the following day to the mining village. There were two launches in the party, as a number of party members from both the Lokko and Sagresa branches came along with me to lend their help. The launch I was in was much the faster; and within an hour of leaving the jetty at Sagresa we were being welcomed by a large and certainly very healthy-looking contingent of party members at the mining village. The day was spent in looking carefully into their branch organisation, and advising them as to how to improve and expand it. The members were for the most part very slightly educated manual workers, with a sprinkling of semi-skilled, skilled and, in I believe two cases, managerial staff. Somewhat isolated from the rest of the country, and with hardly any previous experience as to how to manage the affairs of an organisation of this sort, they were almost pathetically grateful for the trouble we had taken to come and help them. I reflected with satisfaction as we left them in the middle of the afternoon that the party would now find the members of this branch amongst is stoutest adherents.

As we walked back to the jetty to board our launches, someone suggested a quick trip to a historic little island nearby before returning to Sagresa. I had never been to this island before, and so although it was cutting things a bit fine if we wanted to make Sagresa before dark, I agreed. It might be a long time before the opportunity to see it presented itself again. So the two launches chugged across to the tiny island, and we all got out and made a quick tour round.

It was a rocky, hilly islet in the middle of the intricate pattern of river tributaries and creeks which make fine lace of the coastline at this point, but seagoing vessels could sail almost up to it. Consequently, for as long as white men had been interested in Songhai, so long had this little bastion been important as a fortified trading post. A large volume of slaves, ivory, and other valuables had flowed through it in exchange for beads, bangles, and other inconsiderable trifles. It had been stormed, burned, rebuilt, demolished, and restored a dozen times; had changed ownership almost as often; and, in a way, had had writ large on its hoary walls the whole turbulent history of the colony since the advent of the white man. The whole place had at this time been converted into a tourists' showpiece: the old cannon were spotless, the thick walls patched up and their feet shaved of weeds, and the courtyard where the unfortunate slaves were once herded like cattle in a pen looked not at all sinister in the reddening afternoon light. Even the graveyard at the other end of the island, kept scrupulously neat and tidy, seemed to belie the terribly disordered history which it had witnessed: the treachery and inhumanities perpetrated by black men against other black men, white men against other white men, and by each race against the other. Now only a careful deciphering of the inscriptions on one or two of the headstones in the graveyard would give a hint of the sordid story; that, and the countless human bones and weapons which must have fallen into the rocky waters round the little islet, and which one fancied might still be found here and there in its shallows.

Yes; altogether a nice quiet retreat, redolent of history and balmy with the scent of shrubs and flowers. And yet I had a strange premonition of evil as we hurried round. It may have been no more than the fact that clouds were piling threateningly overhead, the wind was freshening, and the surface of the water below us was steadily becoming more choppy. The other, slower, launch set off hastily with the bulk of our party, and I was left alone to work on some papers in the smaller and faster craft by which I had travelled up the river that morning.

I had in the launch with me Kwaku, a driver whose services I had engaged about six weeks before. I liked driving, but was finding that my increasingly frequent runs between Lokko and Sagresa were both tiring and time-consuming. At least now they gave me a chance to catch up with some of my reading.

Kwaku had never given me, up to this point, the slightest cause to doubt his loyalty to me. He was a huge, muscular fellow, with a deep unexplained scar over the right eye, somewhat uncommunicative, and at times even surly. But he was also a very good driver, careful as well as expert, and one who took intense pride in the appearance of his vehicle. It was far below his dignity, of course, to have anything to do with the maintenance and servicing of its mechanical parts, and he would not touch an oilcan or pump with a barge pole. But woe betide any urchin who so much as left a fingerprint on the wax finish of the bodywork after Kwaku had cleaned it.

Kwaku had, as far as my knowledge went, only the usual vices and virtues of drivers in any country. As I sat in the tiny cabin of the launch, half lulled to sleep by the cradlelike motion she developed as she sliced swiftly through the waves running across her bows, I shook off determinedly my sense of unease. Turning on all the cabin lights, I tried to force myself to read through some copies of the local *Hansard* I had brought along. In spite of all I could do, however, *Hansard* proved an effective sedative, and I soon dozed off.

Silence can wake just as effectively as noise. The sudden cessation of the rocking movement and of the noise from the engine, and the dying off of the crash of waves on the launch's hull penetrated my consciousness. I woke with a start to find that we were adrift in the broad creek. Driving rain was sweeping toward us from astern, through the porthole the lights of Sagresa were still alarmingly distant, and low clouds were almost scraping their bellies against the top of our mast.

'What's up, Kwaku?' I shouted up the companionway.

'De engine don die, masta.'

'Well, you both hurry up and fix it.'

No reply; and there had been a peculiar edge to Kwaku's voice which I did not like. The sound of halfhearted tinkering came from the little engine room for'ard of the cabin. I started up the steep flight of steps up onto the deck, and bumped into Kwaku coming down them.

'De fitter say e no get de right tool for fix engine.' Kwaku could speak Hausa, and I think the broken English which he was using, when he knew perfectly well I preferred him to speak Hausa, annoyed me quite as much as what he said.

'Now listen, Kwaku. You are a driver; he is a fitter or a mechanic or something. Between you you must find the tools and get this boat going quick, or I sack you and report him as soon as we land.'

Kwaku looked at me sullenly for a moment, turned and went back up the steps. I heard his footsteps shuffling for'ard, and a muttered conversation take place between him and the man who was tinkering with the engine. I hauled myself up on deck; the waves were breaking over the stern of the launch from time to time, the navigation lights were describing weird arcs against the sky, and the darkness all around us was growing ever more intense. We were drifting fast, and I began to feel the first quivers of fear – fear of rocks, sand-banks, crocodiles, of being carried out to sea. I have never been a brave man; and I think even a brave man might have felt apprehensive in such a situation. The relentless rain was soaking through my clothes, and I retreated again to my cabin, praying desperately that my crew should be given the wisdom and skill to get the launch going again soon.

In fact, I was soon to discover that it was neither wisdom nor skill they wanted, but something quite different. Kwaku's bare legs padded down the companionway, with little rivulets of water running down them. When his head appeared below the hatch, there was an ugly expression on his face.

'De fitter say, if you go do something for im e go try for find de tools.'

My first assumption was that I was being bribed; that Kwaku was being sufficiently disloyal to me to join with the mechanic of the launch in taking advantage of our predicament to get some money out of me. It was an irritating thought; but it did offer some glimmer of hope that they might really tackle in earnest the job of getting the engine going again.

I swallowed my indignation painfully. 'Tell your friends

there that I will give them a good dash if they get me to the quay in half an hour.'

Kwaku looked me unblinkingly in the eyes. 'No be dash e want, sir.'

The full significance of this statement took a few seconds to register in my mind. I waited incredulously.

'E say Mr Wright be im brother. E say if you go promis say you go help Mr Wright, e go try for help you now for make we reach to Sagresa.'

So that was it. I suddenly felt seasick, then very cold. Mr Wright and his friends were pursuing their aims in this foul way. Kwaku had probably been looking out for an opportunity like this for some days now. Disconnected thoughts chased each other across my mind. I wonder how much they have paid Kwaku for this. Anyhow, it must be less than he has paid the crew of the launch, mustn't it? Could I swim for it? How would they force me to keep my promise if I did give in?

'Do, masta, you go try sign dis paper quick, le we go try look for de tools.'

Above all, I realised, I must keep up the appearance of dignity and composure, whatever I was feeling like inside. 'Kwaku,' I abandoned English for Hausa, 'I have trusted you for many days now to look after me. You have had my life in your hands every day. You have never let me down. That is why I brought you along with me in this launch. When I have trusted you so much, what you are doing now is very wicked.'

No reply.

'What paper is that you want me to sign?'

'As for me, masta, A no sabi book; Me no know waitin de na de paper. But A sabi coppo. Waitin dem pay me fo do, na dat A de do. Mesef want small coppo.'

'Stop speaking broken English. You know I don't like it. Speak your own language.'

Stolidly, he repeated his explanation in Hausa, and somehow the words sounded more reasonable: 'I can't read, sir; I don't know what's on this paper. But I do know money. I am doing what I have been paid to do. I too want a little money.'

Even the halfhearted tinkering had stopped by now, and I imagined that the mechanic in the engine compartment, waiting for the result of Kwaku's mission, realised with sound psychological instinct the demoralising effect on me of complete silence in a situation such as this. And yet, strange to say, my courage was gradually returning, and I felt much further from panic than I had a few minutes earlier. I glanced out of the porthole. There was absolutely nothing to be seen now except the trickles of water running down the outside of the glass. The rays from the launch's navigation lights, finding nothing at all to reflect them, were swallowed up immediately by the profound gloom – if indeed they were now on at all. I held out a hand.

'You can't expect me to sign without reading it, Kwaku.'

'It is not the wish of the man who wrote it that you should read it, sir.'

I realised that if this was a written undertaking to bring about the merger of my party with the N.U.C., to sign it now and then break the undertaking later on the ground that it had been made under duress was the obvious course. On the other hand it might not be a document of that nature at all. The instructions given to Kwaku that I was not to read the paper strengthened my suspicions that it was something quite different. It seemed to me that he had probably been told to try first of all to get an oral promise from me that I would effect the desired merger. We who have for countless centuries had to rely on each other's word of mouth for promises and undertakings of all types attach far more weight to an oral guarantee than do other peoples. Once we have given our word, we do not easily break it. Kwaku's principals were perhaps relying naïvely in the first instance on this fact; and hoping that in my initial fright at my predicament I would make such an oral promise.

Kwaku, however, had not persisted very long on this course. The signing of the mysterious document, intended probably only as a last resort, seemed to have been demanded by him of me somewhat prematurely. Perhaps he wished to secure as soon as possible this tangible proof of success in his mission for presentation when he went to claim the balance of his bribe.

If only, I thought desperately, I could get a glimpse of the contents of the paper. It was doubly demoralising not to have any idea to what I was being forced to commit myself, or the P.U.L.

'Kwaku, if you don't know how to read, how will you know whether I have signed my own name?' I asked, hoping that this loophole had been overlooked.

He drew another sheet of paper from his trouser pocket. I recognised it as a Labour Department form which all employers of registered labour in the country had to sign in respect of each of his employees, and which was kept by the employee. Silently, he scanned first one side of the form, then the other, his brows puckered with the effort of concentration. Finally, he found what he was looking for; and poked a mahogany finger at what I recognised, even at that carefully maintained distance, to be my own signature.

'Man teaches man to read; God teaches man just to see. The eyes God gave me will look at the two signatures, and tell me whether they are the same.' Kwaku seemed slightly contemptuous of my failure to realise that this course was open to him.

In a moment, I had come to my decision. It is all very well, of course, to sit in a comfortable armchair and say that I ought to have called Kwaku's bluff. But it must be remembered that Songhai was then, and still is, a country in which one of its natives could very easily lose himself. I could not swim well. Kwaku, I knew very well, could swim like a fish, and I was pretty sure that his fellow-conspirator could too, being a waterfront man. If they were being paid sufficiently well for it, they could, without much fear of retribution, have abandoned me on the small craft to drift seawards through the night. At least the ease with which they could with impunity endanger my life in the situation in which we were, seemed to my alarmed mind very great that night. My pretence that I was not afraid was, further, beginning to wear a little thin, as the silent minutes ticked by; and the strangeness and unreality of the position was beginning to tell on me.

I sat down limply, trying hard to pull myself together. 'All right, Kwaku; I'll sign.'

His expression showed little change at his victory.

'Masta, you promise not to talk, too?'

'Yes,' I said, and added to myself, 'You are a far bigger fool than I took you for if you really believe that I, African or no African, will keep *that* promise.'

He padded up the steps, and a few minutes later the engine burst stridently into sound. Half an hour's sailing at top speed across the still turbulent waters of the creek brought us alongside the quay. The launch mechanic, when I was able to dig him out of the engine room, was full of apologies for the 'breakdown' in midstream, which he said only God helped him to rectify when he did. The anxious little group which was waiting for us was treated by him to a dramatic and voluble account of his frantic efforts to repair the engine in a swaying, half-flooded engine room, and with an incomplete set of tools.

But of Kwaku there was no sign at all, although I was up on deck long before the launch reached the side of the jetty. He was showing me that he could after all distinguish between a good risk and a bad. He had slipped silently into the dark water.

168

CHAPTER TWELVE

I SAID NOTHING to anyone except Samuel that evening about my experience, as I had to rush straight from the jetty to keep an important dinner engagement for which I was already late. I planned to call Kai-Kai to Samuel's house (where I was staying) first thing the following morning and go with him to make a report to the police, if he agreed this was the best course.

But by then it was already too late. The six a.m. news bulletin carried 'dramatic revelations'. A letter from me was reported received by the chairman of the N.U.C., proposing the very scheme that Mr Wright had brought me the previous week. A photograph of my letter, it was promised, would appear in the following day's papers.

At the emergency party executive meeting I called, my story was accepted at once. It was recognised however that it would have to be proved to the rest of the party and to the electorate, and quickly. The British officials, at least some of whom must have been mystified next day by the wording of a letter in which I seemed to be proposing, instead of accepting, the bases-for-aid bargain they had already reached with the N.U.C., were saying nothing. Had I made a report to the police as soon as I landed, or at least before the news first broke, it would have been easy to expose the whole plot. But neither Samuel nor I had anticipated that it would mature overnight.

Kai-Kai and Samuel dug out the launch mechanic, who stood by his story that he had seen or heard nothing unusual on board whilst struggling to repair the engine. Finding Kwaku before issuing my statement seemed our only chance.

But the country was large, sparsely populated and thinly policed, and time was running out.

Leaving Samuel and Kai-Kai in Sagresa I drove hastily to Lokko. Kayinde told me at once that Fatmata had sent a message saying she wanted to see me urgently. Her face, as I entered the cell, wore a look that was inquiring rather than reproachful. I told her my story.

'Describe him to me,' she said.

When I finished she said quietly, 'I believe he's here. He was brought in this afternoon for being drunk and disorderly at a customs post up on the border.'

Six months later I was Prime Minister and two of the N.U.C. leaders had joined Kwaku in jail. Fatmata and Samuel, having both served their terms, were now released. Kayinde and I had brought Fatmata home with a pride and affection which, with the news that Kayinde was pregnant, had made Fatmata glow with happiness.

On polling day I had remained in Lokko the whole day, moving from polling station to polling station in a party propaganda van, and satisfying myself that our party members were behaving with orderliness. With so little opposition, I found that, in fact, they were finding it most difficult to work up any excitement at all. In Sagresa there was, by contrast, a sense of suspense. And in both places, as everywhere else in the territory, the European administrative officials supervised with the greatest dignity and efficiency the opening of a door through which they knew they must leave soon after our party had entered.

As soon as the results were announced in Lokko late that night I left by road for Sagresa, arriving at daybreak. There were very few people in the streets on the outskirts of the city; but there was a sizable crowd outside the Community Centre, where the outlying results were being recorded and announced as they were received by telephone from returning officers. From the moment my car was recognised I sensed an increased deference toward me on the part of the police and other officials. I was soon experiencing the indescribable pleasure of watching myself being slowly metamorphosed from a noisome politician, treated with mild contempt by the Law, by Medicine, and by Education (and with active hostility by the Secretariat) into the country's most important citizen. Why should I deny that it gave me such great satisfaction? What new Prime Minister, in the excited, flushed early hours of victory, does not privately preen himself, puff out his chest, and think the world of himself? I know I did.

We met at Samuel's house later that morning, counted our successes, planned our Cabinet, and, more methodically now, framed policy on issues we knew to be of immediate urgency. Samuel had been returned easily, as had most of our other supporters, and we found we could command the support of at least two-thirds of the new House of Representatives. In the middle of the afternoon the telephone rang; and although it was the fiftieth time it had done so that day, something prompted Samuel to say, 'Bet that's the Private Secretary'; and so it was. An hour later I was ushered into the unfamiliar opulence of Goverment House. I was entering it for the first time, and I reflected with a quiet smile that to be offered on my first call there the highest post it was in the power of its occupant to offer was quite an honour. My mind went back to the day many years before when I had stood outside those lofty iron gates as a small boy, just arrived from the bush. I remembered the friendly soldier on sentry duty, who had chatted with me. This time the sentry still did not know who I was as I drove in; he stopped my car whilst he phoned for authority to admit me. Instead of this incident injecting a little much-needed humility into me, it merely caused me to look forward with increased pleasure to seeing what would be the guard's reaction when he finally caught up with the news. This he had obviously done by the time I left, judging from the bone-jarring alacrity with which he sprang to the salute as my car approached this time, and the sheepish grin his eyes gave me on either side of the glinting bayonet.

Sir Horace Montague-Bidborough had an air of exaggerated affability and bonhomie throughout our interview. He did not like the trend of events in West Africa. He was trying, desperately but unsuccessfully, to disguise his dislike for the remaining year of so of service before his well-earned retirement. I remember reflecting that, at the moment, the fact that he was genuinely making such an attempt at dissimulation was far more important than the fact that he had anything to disguise. My proposals for the appointment of ministers and parliamentary secretaries were accepted *en bloc*, details such as the dates and agenda for the House of Representatives meeting were left open; and after a word with the Chief Secretary (who was in attendance throughout) about personal details such as moving into the official Prime Minister's residence and taking over his car, I left to return to Samuel's house and report to my faithful followers.

The next few years saw no dramatic developments in Songhai. It is much more difficult to work miracles in office than to demand them out of it. My happiest hours were spent in the House chamber, listening to Samuel's inexhaustible flow of oratory. The Opposition were not merely outnumbered, but virtually demoralised by this one agency. The rest of us had very little to do in this connection. There were only three honourable members opposite who even tried seriously and consistently to pit themselves against him, and they invariably had the worst of it. His wit and imagination were never more fertile. When all three were present, he would refer to them as Shadrach, Meshach, and Abednego, and produce puns and metaphors *ad lib* about their pathetic plight in the fiery furnace of a West African parliamentary chamber. Yes, the missionaries had made an excellent job of Samuel.

In our offices, however, I think all of us were much less at ease. This was certainly not the fault of our permanent officials, who, in the best British traditions, served all their political masters 'with equal impartiality and equal contempt'. But each of us had found a bureaucratic web of such intricacy in his portfolio that even to unravel it entailed a long and taxing mental exercise. We spent hours on end during the day being shown round the various government departments under our authority, looking very wise and feeling very ignorant. Then we spent almost as many hours at night thumbing our way unenthusiastically through files which we had been assured would give us a clear picture of the problems, plans, and projects for which the whole country now held us responsible. I now saw clearly, for example, that the diamond smugglers had left Songhai bleeding freely from wounds which desperately required closing.

Perhaps however our most uncomfortable moments were those spent at international conferences – not those on political or constitutional matters, which we found right up our street, but those on technical subjects such as medical research or fisheries development. When one of these highly specialised conferences was being held in Sagresa on a matter within one of our portfolios, we ought, of course, to have attempted no more than the formal opening of it and the welcoming of the delegates. And when it was held elsewhere, we ought to have contented ourselves with sending our 'experts' to it.

But all the African governments had at this time formed the habit of sending high-powered ministerial delegations to these conferences in each other's territories, with the 'expert' advisers merely 'in attendance'. No cabinet wished to appear less vigilant over the interests of the people than any other elsewhere; so ministerial representatives trooped along every time, and a thoroughly miserable time we usually had of it for our pains.

I well remember one such conference on infant mortality, attended by a dozen tropical African countries. My portfolio at the time included Health; and as I had always wanted to visit the newly independent African republic where it was being held, I set off with a keen sense of anticipation, accompanied by my Chief Medical Adviser, Dr Paulling.

On the way across the infinitely varied shades of green land below us, and whilst Paulling tried, more kindly than successfully, to initiate me into the mysteries of infant mortality, my mind dwelt for the most part on what I knew from hearsay and my general reading about Kanem, the country to which we were going. It was regarded with much admiration by all of us in Songhai, and I was wondering whether or not I was going to be disappointed.

My first glimpse of Lakeville, its capital, through a window of the banking aircraft was certainly impressive. I could see the untidily coiled necklace of green lagoons; and on their banks, islands, and stretching far into the mainland, a great city. On the outskirts there was, it was true, a shanty-town of considerable size; but in the centre of the town, on Lakeville Island itself, there were some magnificent buildings.

We were met by a flattering array of important people, including the Minister of Health and his Chief Medical Adviser. We were driven through the sprawling untidiness of the outskirts to a recently reclaimed and developed suburb behind the harbour, where lay street after street of attractive bungalows, each set in a neat if small garden. The tall modern commercial blocks hereabouts and the great

174

public buildings on Lakeville Island bore eloquent testimony to the wealth of the country.

As I should have known, however, the conference itself gave me some of the most boring hours I had spent for a very long time, listening to highly technical jargon of which I understood nothing. It was a great relief when, on the second day, my opposite number on the Kanem side of the table drew me aside and suggested that we trust our 'experts' to protect the interests of our electorates as well as advancing the frontiers of medicine. His Prime Minister, whom I had not yet met, had asked if all the visiting heads of the delegation would call on him. Dr Paulling raised his hands in mock alarm when I told him I was leaving him to it.

It was noon when we left the conference hall on the Atlantic Drive for the Prime Minister's official residence not far away. Shops and offices were just emptying, and the narrow, illogically laid-out streets were congested beyond belief. Parking had long since been forbidden on all main streets; parallel yellow lines were supposed, like the carpet in the British House of Commons, to keep potentially hostile forces out of each other's reach. And exceedingly hostile Lakeville traffic seemed to be. You found yourself in a general state of war with all other vehicles, and most of all with the solid phalanxes of billowing-gowned cyclists who wove in and out of their own right of way with the recklessness of horses jockeying for position on the first bend.

When we finally reached him, I found the Kanem Prime Minister to be a man in his late sixties, short and very fat. His hair was liberally streaked with grey now, but his eye was still a pool of limpid twinkles, and there was not a wrinkle on his face. One could sense at once how he got his reputation as a gay blade on the one hand, and a statesman of genius on the other. Known once as an incorrigible Don Juan, he had suddenly startled the whole country by marrying, in middle age, an aged Lakeville matron of doubtful

175

pedigree and even more doubtful morals, whom his many paramours had all mistaken for his housekeeper. On his bachelor's eve a voice suspiciously like his had been heard singing loudly, 'I ain't goin' to sin no more!' from a succession of friends' houses in Lakeville, and he had kept his word. The tragic death of his wife in a motor accident in which they were both involved two months before our conference was reported to have shaken him up badly, physically as well as emotionally.

Indeed from the moment we shook hands I realised that this was a sad and a tired man. I recalled the circumstances of the fatal accident, which had been very fully reported in the Sagresa papers. The P.M. and his wife were at the time being driven at some speed along one of the new trunk roads of which his Government had always been so proud. A big closed van was slowing down ahead of their car, its near-side traffic indicator out as it prepared to turn off into a side road. Their chauffeur, already a little behind schedule, and judging accurately that the van would be out of his path just before he reached it, had kept straight on withou slackening speed. He could not have guessed that, masked by the van, a loaded timber lorry was illegally parked on the main road a few yards beyond the junction, right in his path. An eye-witness had later described how, as the van turned off to reveal the obstruction, the P.M.'s car's stop-lights had flushed crimson with alarm, brakes had screeched in terror, and a violent side-swipe had crumpled the car's near-side body-work, killing Mrs Owoo-Jones on the spot. The driver and the P.M., sitting on the off-side, had escaped with bruises and severe shock.

Those flashing eyes excepted, it was a man of serious mien and few words who waved us to our seats. 'Well, gentlemen,' he said, as soon as we were served with drinks, and had exchanged courtesies, 'there is something I want to take the opportunity of discussing with you while you are here – just to sound you out on it, you know; no records of our talk to be made, none of our governments to be committed in any way, quite informal. To come to the point at once, I've been wondering whether we are not yet ready to start planning for a United States of Africa, some kind of federation of our territories.'

He paused for a moment and watched carefully the effect of his words. Then, 'I believe in candour,' he added. 'A few years ago I should not have suggested it – we have been too busy putting our own house in order. But now that our countries are all independent or nearly so, and are also prosperous, secure and well-ordered, is the matter not worth thinking about?'

'We have always looked forward to your showing more interest in this matter,' a minister from another republic said, leaning forward eagerly.

'We have discussed it vaguely at party level,' I added, not to be outdone, 'and, subject to proper safeguards for the interests of small states, I am sure my government would be only too pleased to co-operate fully with you.' But what I was thinking was, 'I wonder just how many times similar hopes have been expressed on similar occasions during the past few years.'

Then suddenly we all realised that this time it was different. I think it was something in our host's manner as he smiled in a kind of serious satisfaction, and then fumbled in a drawer for a sheet of paper. In silence he read it through to himself, as if to refresh his memory as to its contents. Then he handed it to us saying, 'Here's something else I wanted to discuss with you – something not altogether unrelated to what I've just said.' It was a letter bearing an address in Johannesburg.

Dear Mr Owoo-Jones:
   This is a cry from Macedonia. You know how the whites

here have prostituted both the Constitution and the Judiciary of South Africa in order to keep the natives and coloured people in virtual serfdom in separate states with so-called 'home-rule'. We have tried to fight back by constitutional means over many years, but without success. Our plight, instead of improving, is worsening year by year. You elsewhere in Africa are now in control of your own affairs. We your cousins in the Republic of South Africa now appeal to you to remember that, before the white man came, there were no political frontiers between your country and ours, and many links of blood and culture. If you do not hear our cry and help us, there is no other people in the world who will, and we shall give up hope altogether.

What we request is that your political parties make us a loan of ten million pounds. This money would be used to finance a last desperate campaign, whose ultimate aim will be to create a truly multi-racial society in this Republic, with all races living together in real social equality. We admit that South Africa is now as much the home of the whites as it is ours. We do not wish to exterminate or even expel the whites. We wish instead to organise a mass withdrawal of native labour and custom from all white-owned enterprises in the Republic, including the mines. The whites here want our money and our labour, but not our votes or our company. We propose to compel them to choose between having all these and having none. On a day to be decided later, we shall cripple every mine, farm, and commercial house in the Union by a nation-wide boycott.

But, in order to achieve success, you will understand that this project must be most carefully prepared. A vast publicity campaign must be launched, so that no black home in the Republic is ignorant of what is being done, and what are the issues at stake. We already have a nation-wide organisation representing native interests. But it must be greatly enlarged and reinforced, to make sure that the message reaches everybody. All we ask for is a loan – a loan with which to finance our campaign, and to establish a resettlement fund out of which to make our people once more self-supporting on the land, in our own reserves, to which they will withdraw if this becomes necessary. We believe we shall be able to repay you one day. With God's help, our cause will be successful; and our beloved country will become what God meant it to be – a place where all of us, His children, whatever our colour, may have a margin to our lives.

> We await with utmost anxiety your reply,
> Your cousins in distress . . .

Here followed three signatures above the respective designations of Chairman, Secretary, and Treasurer of the South African Native Congress.

The P.M.'s eyes were fixed on me when I looked up, and then they moved to the other faces around the room, as one by one each person read the letter silently. I was strangely excited. I remembered seeing a picture somewhere of ruined white businesses in Tuskegee, Alabama, and in Buganda, Uganda – ruined irretrievably by well-organised boycotts of the Negro majority which each population contained. There was no more inexorable way of bringing an intolerant minority to its knees without blood-letting. Just as it would be even more effective, so too would it be far more costly and difficult to organise such a boycott throughout South Africa. But they were right. It clearly was ultimately only a matter of organisation, and of money. Then, I thought, South Africa again – why must my footsteps be constantly dogged by race relations down there? Why, at every important juncture of my life, must affairs in that unhappy land obtrude themselves across my path? Was I fated to become personally involved in some way or other in South African affairs, whether I wished it or not? I knew now I could not honestly say I did not wish it. A picture of Friedrik's giant figure snarling angrily in that Keswick hotel came to my mind. In spite of myself, I hated his guts. Then I fought and conquered the revulsion and felt better. And still it seemed as if the call from Macedonia were addressed to me personally, as if Mr Owoo-Jones were but the messenger of Fate, as if something within me recognised that my life purpose was at last being revealed to me in its entirety.

'Well?' our host was asking, after a considerable period of silence. 'What is your first reaction? No commitment, of course.'

'I daren't even tell you without consulting my colleagues. Too important a matter,' someone said, and this view found echoes all round the room.

'And you, Mr Kamara? Care to say anything about it at this stage?'

I hesitated still. I realised that the reply I had just heard was the only reasonable one.

'I understand the circumspection which you show.' Mr Owoo-Jones' eyes were disarmingly smiling. 'You will realise however that our own interests in this matter coincide very closely with those of the natives of South Africa. By drawing closer to them we shall be, in a very real sense, drawing closer to each other too; and nobody can deny that that's a very good thing in itself. This is a heaven-sent peg on which to hang the disordered strands of African nationalism, and so prepare for the establishment of the federal African state I believe we all look forward to creating. But that I propose we make the subject of a Pan-African Conference.'

In a flash I realised that this was, for our host, the supremely important aspect of this matter. I wondered whether he were cherishing a secret ambition to become the first Prime Minister of a United States of Africa. The domestic history of each African territory in recent years had shown clearly that, to use Mr Owoo-Jones' metaphor, there was no better peg on which to hang disparate political material than a common enemy. The British had always played that rôle with unintended effectiveness in North America, in the Far East, in the Middle East, and now in Africa. I looked at the pleasant face before me, in which impatience had begun to cloud over the amiability with which my reply was awaited. I knew at last what I must say. However different our motives might be, Mr Owoo-Jones and I were from now on fellow-crusaders in the same cause. It was as if he had reminded me of a mission I had forgotten, no doubt because my conscious mind recognised that it would be a difficult and unpleasant one.

I stretched out my hand impulsively and took his. 'I give you my word that I, with or without the support of my government, will do everything within my power both to bring about a United States of Africa, and to help our brothers in South Africa to do what they have set out in this letter to achieve.'

They were all clearly taken aback by my fervour. I remember that quite clearly, though I have forgotten exactly how they showed their surprise, or even what was our next topic of conversation.

CHAPTER THIRTEEN

I STEPPED DOWN the gangway from the plane and kissed Kayinde warmly. 'Fatmata sends you her welcome,' she assured me. I turned to the little group of civil servants and ministerial colleagues waiting near by, and shook their welcoming hands. I was assured that everything was in order, and thanked God privately that there would be no distracting subject at the party executive meeting which I intended to call at once.

We met that very evening in my house. It was, as usual, a very informal meeting, with coffee, biscuits, sandwiches and soft drinks circulating. I gave a brief report on the mission on which I had gone, and then summarised the contents of the South African letter. (We had agreed not to make any copies, as it was essential that the whole matter should be treated as highly confidential at this stage.)

Characteristically, it was Samuel who spoke first.

'I'm all in favour, and I hope everyone else is too. We let ourselves down if we let those people down.'

'What about details such as the distribution of this loan burden between the creditors?' someone asked. 'Did Mr Owoo-Jones say anything about that?'

'No, he didn't. I think he is leaving all details until agreement in principle is reached. He did say, however, that he is hoping this might be the first step in a closer association between African states. He said something about calling a Pan-African Conference to work out the details and to discuss "other matters of mutual interest", as he put it, if all parties signify their approval in principle.'

'Wouldn't mind going to South Africa myself to help organise the boycott,' Samuel said.

It was intended as a joke, of course; but somehow that remark stuck in my mind. We agreed to signify to Mr Owoo-Jones our approval of the loan project 'in principle', but I felt strangely dissatisfied as I went about my crowded business. I knew that I had a personal duty to do beyond merely persuading my colleagues to agree to co-operate. I waited impatiently to hear from Lakeville about other reactions, and when word came that other governments too were favourable, Samuel's remark about playing a personal part in the campaign returned to me with redoubled force. I was certain that I had once more been shown my own path of duty. Day after day that conviction grew on me with overwhelming certainty.

On a sudden impulse I sought Fatmata's advice. Perhaps it was her unflinching fidelity to me and my interests that made me do it; perhaps it was simply my absolute faith in her good sense and shrewd judgment. She considered a long time in silence when I stopped talking that evening in my bedroom.

'Do you trust Samuel absolutely?' she asked unexpectedly at last.

'Yes, Fatmata. Of course. Why?'

'If so, I believe that is proof that it is Allah's will you should go to South Africa and leave affairs here in his hands until you return.' Her directness, her economy of words, were never more characteristic of her than on this occasion.

Even then I was reluctant to accept it as finally and inescapably my fate that I should go south ostensibly to serve the Congress's cause and privately to seek Greta's murderer. But I could not escape the conviction that this I must do the certainty that until I did I should find neither rest nor happiness in anything. And yet I recognised this desire as quite irrational. I had just attained to the highest office a Songhaian could reach; wealth, prestige, power, were all at my command. I had the opportunity to bring a better mode of life to all my fellow citizens, not only by my work in their interest, but also by my personal example in private and public life. I had a supremely happy home life, and a cherished circle of friends.

In exchange, what might I achieve, even if the South African Native Congress's ambitious plans matured? I should probably help the inscrutable Mr Owoo-Jones to mount another rung up the ladder of his ambitions (which might of course be an excellent thing if in the process the peoples of Africa were brought closer together). If I returned safely from South Africa, my mission successfully completed, I should, it is true, command unequalled personal popularity. And how easily my wife had assumed that I *should* return safely. 'Leave affairs here in his hands until you return,' she had said confidently. But what were my chances of returning safely? I should be marked out, from the moment the whole affair became public, for the special hostility of the South African government. And that there might be tension and unrest during the campaign amongst the natives themselves as well as between them and the whites, I thought highly likely. A whole population is not led so easily to give up the social and occupational habits of generations.

And yet some power greater than my own will and my own instincts was forcing me to go, and I could not resist.

My decision once made to resign after my present term of office, I felt quite unexcited. There was a budget session on just about that time, and we were all very fully occupied with its business.

The weeks and then the months ran past, and the date Mr Owoo-Jones had now fixed for the Pan-Africa Conference approached. It was to be held strictly *in camera*; and although we knew that by now the South African government had almost certainly got wind of what was afoot, an elaborate attempt was to be made to prevent that government obtaining any more details at this stage. The whole of a new two-hundred-room hotel on the coast just outside Lakeville was to be taken over for the occasion. I decided that Samuel and I should represent the P.U.L.

Mr Owoo-Jones' party acted as hosts, and proved excellent organisers. From first to last they set out to impress both the visiting delegates and the watching public with the importance of the occasion. Our plane was met by a large welcoming party headed by five ministers and large numbers of party supporters. We were exempted from customs and immigration formalities; and then shown into the largest American car I have ever set eyes on, whose chromium-plated grin was so wide that you almost grinned back involuntarily. On either side of us a dozen motor-cyclists took up their position, decked in their party colours, while the local police, also on motor-cycles, led the procession. Intensive planning, expense, and publicity had clearly gone into the preparations for our reception, and I could not help wondering what was the real purpose behind all this stunting at a conference whose business was supposed to be secret. Was Mr Owoo-Jones making political capital out of the atmosphere of mystery, or was this his party's normal way of doing things? If the former, who was to be the gainer from it all: his own party vis-à-vis the other parties in his country, or himself in the eyes of the visiting ministers? Or both? Somehow I did not expect to be any the wiser on that point at the end of the conference than at the beginning. My earlier meeting with the Kanem Prime Minister had convinced me that his mind had become, since his wife's death, virtually illegible to others.

But I was to be proved quite wrong. I did find the answer to my question during the conference, and it was not at all what I had expected. It was against the most beautiful and impressive of settings that our host was to be at his most unobtrusive. The hotel had then been in existence for only a year, and it was the finest catering and residential establishment in Africa, intended deliberately to attract the tourist trade. For one thing it had been built in spacious grounds, and the sense of spaciousness had been carefully preserved, no other buildings being allowed within sight of it. The grounds were magnificently laid out and maintained, with lawns, ponds, fountains, and gardens of every description, and the most judicious and artistic use of trees to give shade and proportion to the whole. Each room had a telephone, television, individual air-conditioning, and a private bathroom; and there was a magnificent private beach, with direct access from the hotel terraces. I remembered how, when it was being built, there had been criticism in the press of its scale and extravagance; of its siting and its proposed scale of charges. But it appeared the gloomy prophets had been confounded. The high standard set had itself ensured success by attracting not only travel-weary businessmen with expense accounts, but also the curious from within and without the country.

It was against such a background then, that Mr Owoo-Jones chose to keep himself inconspicuously hidden. He made a speech of welcome, of course; and a brilliantly contrived speech it was, too. The case of the South African native could rarely have been more clearly, more persuasively, presented. But after that he deliberately shunned the limelight. He would not be considered for chairman of any session, or as a main speaker. He listened most attentively to all the speeches and discussions, but made no contribution himself. The guest delegates, already a little overawed by everything, particularly by the superb stage management of the whole show, were now visibly and audibly moved to wonder at the modesty of their chief host. Was the actor merely as efficient as his stage managers?

The fact was that Mr Owoo-Jones was quite deliberately trying to avoid taking any more political responsibilities. Since this conference I have maintained that they wrong politicians who say that they are as a profession unprincipled opportunists. The most successful of them, those whom the history books later will call statesmen, *do* have sets of principles to which they remain true, and which are not necessarily dictated by their own interests. This much was clearly shown during that conference. For as it proceeded, and it became clear that practically all the delegates present favoured meeting the Congress's request, our thoughts turned together to the future of the whole continent.

Samuel was the chairman at the crucial session. We had just agreed that the loan to the Congress should be met by all political parties represented at the conference, not by governments. We had agreed on a formula for working out the distribution of the loan burden – a formula based on the total number of paid-up members in each party. This, ostensibly the chief business of the conference, out of the way, the expected question soon came up, from an East African delegate as it happened: 'Was this to be the last conference of this type? Could not a permanent body be set up here and now to convene future ones as need arose?' Then Samuel – not usually a very good chairman, but this time catching the mood of his meeting most accurately, said, 'Why just a series of conferences? Why can't we be bold and draw up proposals now for a federation of African States?'

There was silence for a few seconds; but somehow you could tell that it was the silence of approval, not of hostility. And then one after the other support for the idea was voiced all round the table. A working committee was to be set up at once to study the matter and report to the next conference. Samuel suggested a coffee break before inviting nominations for chairman of the committee.

I felt a tug at my sleeve, and Mr Owoo-Jones was drawing me onto one of the patios. 'Look here, Kamara, it's up to you to take the lead now. you know. If we allow delegates from the larger countries to dominate the scene, we'll scare off the smaller ones. Let me propose your name for this office.'

'What about yourself?' I retorted. 'This is all the result of your initiative.'

He remained silent for a moment. Then he said in a level voice, 'I have important personal reasons for not wishing to do more just now than see the whole thing safely launched.'

'I've noticed you are doing your damndest not to get caught up too fully with it. I take it you would prefer not to tell me why, if your reasons are personal.'

'Oh, I don't know that they are really secret.' He was smiling again, but the smile seemed slow and tired – or was it I who was associating it with his words? 'I'm getting on,' he said. 'I don't know exactly how many years I could give you, but I should think very few. And since my wife died, I've not been the same man. Something vital has gone out of me. You need young men for your new state, not old; vigour, industry and vision, rather than the tragic broodings and half-forgotten experience of grey-heads. I shall be available in the rôle of elder statesman if wanted. That's my proper place. And of course I shall remain at the head of affairs at home as long as my party wishes. But that's the job from which I'd like to retire.'

I glanced quickly at him, as the usually firm voice quavered slightly. I knew at once that nothing would move him from the attitude he had taken up. Ought I to disclose to him my own plans? It was very tempting to do so, but in the end I decided against it. Asking him to give me a few minutes to decide, I sought Samuel and drew him onto a terrace seat.

Apart from Fatmata, I had told no one of my intention to resign after my present term of office. But as circumstances seemed unexpectedly to be forcing me into a situation from which I knew I should have to extricate myself within the year, I felt that the man who would be most deeply affected by such a step should without further delay be admitted into my secrets.

There was a cool breeze blowing off the sea, and the royal palms studding the terrace were in considerable agitation. As fully as I could, without referring to Friedrik, I told Samuel my plans, and tried to convey to him my conviction that the call I heard was undeniable. He accepted this, to my surprise, with very little question. But the possibility that I might not return, that he should take over permanently from me so soon, he would not countenance. And Mr Owoo-Jones' attitude to the leadership of the embryo federation the down-to-earth Samuel found quite incredible.

'If he feels he is too old, why does he not suggest that one of his own colleagues take the lead? Doesn't that sound odd to you?'

It did, now that he had mentioned it. But I said, 'Oh, I believe that old age often brings mistrust of those immediately round you. Anyhow we are thinking too far ahead. The United States of Africa is a long way from being in existence. It's just someone to shoulder the main burden of planning for it that we want at present.'

I had never found it very hard to convince Samuel of anything. He mumbled thoughtfully, 'I did hear Owoo-Jones tell his Minister for Air yesterday that he was considering changing his title to 'Minister for Hot Air', as he had produced more words than planes. But I thought he was only joking, for everybody laughed – including the unfortunate minister concerned.'

'He probably was half-joking,' I said. 'He has a reputation for administering sugared pills.'

Samuel relapsed into silence. I could see that he was fighting an inner struggle with himself over some issue. I tried to guess what it was. Had he too now become conscious of how small were my chances of returning from this apparently senseless venture, or was he diffident about his ability to carry on without me? He had come to rely very heavily on me and my judgment in all kinds of matters during our long friendship, matters of state as well as more personal ones. I guessed he was feeling like a cripple whose crutches are being kicked from under him with his own consent. If so, I knew what approach to make.

'Don't worry about your own ability to hold the fort, old boy. I'm far too patriotic to take on a thing like this if I were not absolutely sure about you on that score.'

It was little more than a shot in the dark, but I had hit the target. Samuel started out of his brown study and gave me a self-defensive, apologetic look. It was the kind of look that he always wore when caught out on something. The last time I had seen it appear was when I had called at his bungalow a few days after he had become a minister, and had found him dutifully feeding the baby, whilst his wife was cooking. She was a true Sagresan girl, strong-willed and eloquent, wielding far more authority in her home than her husband ever succeeded in wielding in his Ministry. On this particular occasion, Samuel had evidently received strict instructions that the baby was to finish every drop of milk in a depressingly large feeding-bottle. He swore later that he had spent half an hour unsuccessfully trying to press the rubber teat between tightly clenched gums. However that may be, it is certain that as I stepped unannounced into the dining-room I had caught a desperate Samuel drinking surreptitiously the contents of the offending bottle, a wary eye cocked in the direction of the kitchen door.

'*Touché*?' I asked gently now.

'How did you guess?' He sounded almost rueful.

'One does pick up a hint or two of a friend's habits of thought in so many years' acquaintance,' I said. 'If that's what is causing all this heart-searching, the search ends here. You've got three times as much gumption in you – and I don't know how much more statesmanship – as those fools who were running our government before we came on the scene. You'll take both the job at home and this federal business in your stride. Look here; I've discovered that the whole secret of this job is to choose your advisers carefully. Once you've done that you just take their advice, that's all. And you are as good a judge of men as I've met.'

Tears were glistening in Samuel's eyes as he turned to me now. He was not the sentimental, sloppy type; but something had touched him deeply. I never found out what. It may have been my expression of confidence in him, for he would probably value that more highly than a K.C.M.G.; or else it may have been the thought of the coming separation.

'I'll do it, Kisimi,' he said very quietly.

'Good chap. I knew you would. You won't regret it. Now let's get back quickly.'

Neither of us spoke again until we were back in our seats in the hall where the resumed session had just started. I found an empty seat behind Mr Owoo-Jones.

'I've decided to stand,' I said in his ear.

'That's wonderful news, Kamara.'

'But only provided that if, for any reason, I have to drop out of politics before the next conference, whoever succeeds me in the job in Songhai also succeeds me in the committee chairmanship.'

He turned and looked at me intently, curiously. 'You've got a foreboding or something?'

'Not exactly a foreboding. Can't say any more just now; but is it agreed?'

'Yes, of course. Perfectly sensible condition, in fact.'

Next morning my photograph was on the front pages

from Cairo to the Cape. Since the South African loan question had not been made public, the setting up of the Standing Closer Committee, as we had agreed to call it, was the only crumb of news the press had so far got out of the conference; and they pecked it up greedily. 'FUTURE AFRICAN FEDERATION PLANNED FOR' the headlines proclaimed. 'SONGHAI P.M. HEADS NEW COMMITTEE.' It was the first time our little territory had received such publicity, and certainly the first time that I had figured so prominently in the outside press.

So I will not deny that Samuel and I were quite overjoyed at the publicity; and we gave carefully phrased interviews to all the numerous pressmen who now sought them. I have an album full of press cuttings of that period, and can still recapture some of the pleasure we derived from reading them.

And so we returned home to Sagresa, home to a phalanx of shutter-happy cameramen, a double brass-band reception, and heart-warming cheers from the crowds lining the streets all the way into town. It felt wonderful to be alive. It was not until I was resting in my bedroom after lunch on the Saturday of our return that I began to feel again those vague flutters of doubt at the wisdom of my own decision to leave all this security and popularity on an apparently senseless mission. I felt the need to rethink out by myself my present situation and future plans, and perhaps to try to rid myself of this persistent call, which had never left me since Samuel had spoken those half-jesting words.

I drove out alone to a nearby beach and walked along that long, curving golden scimitar which forever forbids the blue ocean from invading the green land. I walked half its length and back; and it was so dark when I again reached the place where I had left my car that I had some difficulty in finding it. I was struggling against something – or at least I felt that I was standing aside and watching two claimants fighting for possession of my soul. I was in fact witnessing a struggle between my instinct, which was striving to follow a light within me, and my intelligence, which was trying to assert its right to do what it had selected as socially correct and personally profitable. But it was a struggle intelligence was doomed to lose, for, just as true beauty is in the eye of the beholder, so is true morality in his heart, not his head.

After this afternoon of introspection I never worried again about the future. I went about my task normally, even happily, to the surprise of Samuel, I think. He on the other hand was depressed and moody, and sometimes gave me far more cause for anxiety than did my own future.

In the course of the fairly voluminous secret correspondence which now began passing between the leaders of the South African Native Congress and my Committee on matters connected with the loan, I asked as casually as I could whether the Congress wished for any help other than financial – whether it would like any trained personnel, for example, to help in organising the campaign. The reply came back by return air mail; and to my discomfiture it was a firm but polite negative. I wrote again, this time making a more definite proposal to the effect that such a large sum of money as we were sending required expert handling and careful accounting for. I added that many of the organisations lending the money were experienced in organising big political campaigns. We should be only too pleased to place at the Congress's disposal the services of anyone who might be of any help to them. This time the reply was quite uncompromising. This, said the Congress leaders, was their quarrel, no one else's. They were asking us for a loan, not a gift. They did not deny their relative inexperience in launching widespread popular campaigns of this type. But in insisting that they should manage the whole business themselves they were seeking above all to confine the tensions within the Republic, and not to involve the rest of Africa more than necessary at this stage. The Republican Government could do nothing about a private loan to the Congress from a group of other political parties. But if it were able to lay hands on a foreigner coming to South Africa on such a mission as I proposed, its vindictiveness would know no bounds. Would I please let them know whether it was impossible for the loan to be made without any strings attached?

They were absolutely right, of course. This was in truth none of our business. But the effect of this letter was to send me into a mood of deep dejection. I felt frustrated, not relieved. I still could not doubt for an instant that I should go to South Africa. But it was clearly going to be much more difficult to carry out my mission than I had at first anticipated. I should have to circumvent the opposition of the Congress to my journey, in addition to facing the certain hostility of the Republican Government. But I could not help myself now. A magnet was drawing me irresistibly on, and each difficulty that faced me merely presented me with yet another challenge to be met and answered.

I now began to scheme and plot for a secret journey southwards. I ordered some Bantu Linguaphone records and I worked away at the language in every spare moment I had until I was satisfied that I could understand, and make myself understood in, a simple Bantu dialogue. From time to time, as I worked through the course, I would come across words that sounded and meant almost the same as words in my own language; and these discoveries always afforded me the greatest pleasure.

English had taken me years of hard work to master; now, although my brain was older and less alert, I mastered Bantu in months. Next I studied with the greatest care the geography of South Africa. The Republic had been divided up some years before this into a checkerboard pattern of reserves, some (always on the best land) for whites; others for natives, Cape coloureds, and Asiatics. Movement from one reserve to another was strictly controlled. 'Separate but equal' and 'Home rule for each race' had been the slogans. But in fact, as all the world knew, it had been nothing more than an elaborate and vicious device for perpetuating the wretchedness of the non-whites.

Amongst my maps was one produced by the Congress which showed with startling clarity the extent to which white South Africans were making a hollow mockery of the 'separate but equal' doctrine. I marvelled as I gazed at this Congress map at the skill with which it had been devised; and I was now sorry that in my earlier letter I had pretended to doubt the capacity of these people to produce marvels of organisaiton when put to the test. For as yet they had very little money available. We had agreed, for reasons of security, secrecy, and convenience, that the loan should be sent to the Congress in a series of monthly instalments. These were to be spread over a period of more than a year, each instalment being in effect the contribution of one of the subscribing political parties, sent by the party itself direct to the Congress headquarters. The Standing Closer Committee merely received from the parties concerned advice that the remittances had been sent and received.

So there could not yet have been a great deal of money to spend on this map. Yet it succeeded in being both a work of art and a mine of information. The reserves were shown in appropriate colours – black for native areas, brown for 'coloured' areas, yellow for Asiatic areas, and white for 'white areas'. Graphs, diagrams and figures showed at a glance the number of schools and hospitals in each type of reserve per million of the population, the productivity of the land, the availability of water, and the total expenditure per head from Republican funds. Nothing could have shown as vividly the extent to which *apartheid* in practice was ensuring that the Republicans' hewers of wood and drawers of water would remain so all their lives. The Congress's publicity campaign was off to a most effective start.

I pored over that map until I knew all its details by heart. What use the knowledge was going to be to me I could not guess, but I felt somehow that it was essential that I should arm myself in every way I could for the venture ahead. I read every book and encyclopædia article about the Republic that I could lay hands on. A number of Bantu songs had been imported into Songhai during the preceding years and had achieved a quite remarkable popularity when adapted for dancing. I found in the recordings a welcome additional source of words and idioms.

The South African Native Congress published a full statement of their plans during the very month in which our party's first term in office in Songhai was due to end, and fresh general elections were pending. I knew that the time had come to leave. The Congress had not published the actual date of the start of the mass boycott, but they had sent it to me under top-secret cover. It was planned that, in order to give the boycott its full impact, the date should be announced to native and white alike in South Africa by a midnight drum message.

Before I set out on my journey, however, I had an important call to make. Announcing that I was going on a tour of my constituency, I left Sagresa for Lokko. I wanted my parents' blessing on my venture to add to my wife's; and to seek their opinion as to whether I was doing right, and whether I should return. Strange, it will no doubt appear, how confident I was that they would know the answers.

In all these busy years I had only visited Lokko once before as Prime Minister, and I had forgotten the enthusiasm of the town's welcome. The whole population was out, and that of several other communities too. The car was left a mile out of the village, and I walked in in the centre of a noisy, dusty, straggly procession. My father had moved to a large house befitting his new status and his greatly improved circumstances. Relatives of Ministers and Prime Ministers never want for gifts, I suppose; genuine, well-intentioned gifts, given as compliments, not as bribes. But in other ways he had changed little, hardly seeming even to have aged very much more. As soon as opportunity offered for a talk alone with him I told him briefly of my plans. I said that I was about to leave for another country elsewhere in Africa, to help in some work which would enable our fellow-Africans in that country to take over control of their own affairs just as we had done in our country. Did he approve? After a considerable period of silent reflection, he did. And he added, without my asking, that he knew Allah would bring me back to him safely. And I knew immediately that Allah would. Easily, we passed on to other topics.

That evening a letter arrived for me from the South African Native Congress. The Republican government there had apparently registered its first public reaction by issuing a brief pamphlet, repeating the familiar argument that most of the so-called 'native' tribes had in fact arrived in the Republic a a date subsequent to that of the first white immigrations. None of the race problems facing the Republic, it argued, could be solved if the fact were ignored, that there were no historical reasons for regarding any one of the present racial groups in the Republic as exclusively native to the country.

The Congress reproduced in full the text of this pamphlet, together with their own published reply; and once again I marvelled at the force and cogency of their arguments. The present boundaries of the Republic, they replied, were foreign-imposed and so entirely artificial, as were most boundaries in Africa today. For uncounted centuries, the various tribes of negroes whose home was on the African continent had moved freely from place to place within that continent, as climatic factors, economic pressures and inter-tribal warfare dictated. Bantus, Bushmen, Hottentots; all had been involved in these age-old peregrinations. That did not, however, destroy the essential fact that Africa was the true home of the negro, as Europe was the true home of the white man. To draw an arbitrary political boundary across the southern tip of the African continent, settle colonies of foreigners on that tip, and then say that an African tribe which crossed that boundary subsequently was not native to the country was to fly in the face of all reason. Would, say, the British allow themselves to be treated as foreigners in a previously uninhabited corner of their island on which a group of immigrant West Indians, for example, had decided to settle?

Nevertheless, the Congress reply reasserted, it regarded this distinction between natives and immigrants as of largely academic interest. It was aiming at abolishing *apartheid* in South Africa, not white settlement. Its campaign was directed at securing for all the present inhabitants of the Republic equality of opportunity, education and political rights, irrespective of their race. Whatever the history of the country, it believed that such equality was what its future required, and that the alternative to the securing of this equality would be bloody chaos.

Now, with all the leisure I could wish for temporarily mine, I studied this pamphlet with the greatest care, until I could pretty well recite it by heart. I lay back in the cool of the evening, in the yielding, gently swaying comfort of a hammock under a mango tree, the very same hammock as had swung so many years ago from the veranda roof in our old house. A glow of satisfaction and pleasure filled me, and of vicarious pride too, I think, on behalf of the authors of the Congress's pamphlet. The word 'native', used for so long as a term of contempt, almost of abuse, had now been restored with consummate adroitness to its original meaning, and exploited therein to the utmost. And yet it was not being done vindictively, nor spitefully. The natives of South Africa were still offering their white guests not violence, but equality under the law.

CHAPTER FOURTEEN

THE FIRST thing I did when I woke up next morning was to unfasten the piece of diamond which hung round my neck. I wanted to leave it behind, because I had believed for a long time now that I would die with it on, and I wanted very much to come back, as my father had assured me I should, and die quietly of old age in my own village. I sought out my father in his room.

'Father, I set out on my journey this morning. I shall return soon. But I wish you to keep this stone, which you sent me on the day I was leaving for England. Keep it safe for me; I will surely return for it.'

He said nothing, but merely took the stone and enclosed it in his rough, horny hand. I have often wondered whether he suspected even faintly the type of mission I was undertaking. But how could he possibly have done?

I had already written my letter of resignation to the party executive. I sealed it, gave it to the waiting messenger, and watched him drive off with it. I had stated simply that for 'personal reasons' I did not wish to be nominated again as a candidate, either in the approaching general elections or for the party leadership. I had brought £500 in currency notes with me from Sagresa, and I packed the money in a suitcase, together with the other things I should need and which I had carefully assembled. After a heavy midday meal, and when the whole village was engulfed in the lassitude which the early afternoon heat induces, I slipped out of the back garden with my suitcase. Dodging between the closely packed huts I made my way to the dirt road leading toward the distant frontier. As soon as I thought it safe, I entered the bush, changed into an old pair of shorts and a torn shirt, burned the clothes I had been wearing, shaved my scalp as bald as an egg, and put on a pair of dark glasses. I regained the road, and hailed the first lorry that overtook me. It stopped, and I climbed in gratefully. I bargained with the driver for a minute or two about my fare to the border town, paid him, and then settled in happy exhaustion amongst the chickens and goats on the floorboards of the vehicle. The haggling over the fare had, I hoped, reinforced my disguise; for in no country are Prime Ministers expected to haggle. But I need not have worried. The row of backs bouncing up and down in unison on the narrow wooden seat just behind my head could hardly have looked less suspicious, or even interested. I wondered idly which would have given them the greater surprise, the contents of the battered suitcase on which a number of cracked, leathery soles were now resting, or the identity of the suitcase's owner.

All the rest of that day and all the following night we bounced along, whilst the red dust-clouds swirled shroud-like from beneath the spinning wheels. These mammy-lorries will never change, I thought to myself. They have become a national institution which deserves, like the cable cars of San Francisco, to be protected by the constitution. There was a full moon that night, and the dust-clouds turned silver in its rays when we drove through open country. In forest areas I had the hide-and-seek game of the moon amongst the trees to entertain me, and the frightened cries of the wakened birds winging away into the security and the gloom of the forest on either side. The only stop was to change over from one driver to another, and although I dozed off for a while, my sleep was fitful and unprofitable.

When finally I woke it was broad daylight, and the sight of a large female rump wobbling jellylike up and over the tailboard of the lorry told me that we had just stopped at our destination. I gathered my wits and my belongings as rapidly as I could, and followed the rump overboard. The name on the Postal Agency outside which we had stopped I knew as that of a largish village a mile or two from the border, and the exact place I was making for. With a mumbled word of thanks in the direction of an oil-stained back arched industriously under the lorry's bonnet, I scanned the house fronts up and down the short street for the village shop. It was not far away, and in my suitcase a few tins of joloff rice, egusi sauce, and groundnut stew had soon replaced two of my pound notes. The tins looked as if they were of a ripe old age, and I prayed that the science of hermetic sealing had not yet had to acknowledge defeat in the long struggle to keep their contents fresh. No one was wasting even a second glance on me, so I felt quite secure in my disguise. I sought out a quiet spot in the bush just outside the village, and made an excellent meal of it – my first for nearly twenty-four hours. The food tasted good, washed down with the contents of a small gourd of palm-wine bought from a passing seller.

I do not know how long I then slept; but when I awoke it was late afternoon, and the suitcase under my head had grown hard and uncomfortable. I picked it up and set out for the frontier to reconnoitre. It was a simple affair consisting of a robust barrier, at which a few lorries were drawn up. Officials and passengers stood around. As I had feared, there was little hope of getting through here without identification. In the days when there were no police here it would have been easy. But the police posted here now were centrally recruited and trained, and would all have had a period of service in the capital at some time or other. I dared not risk being recognised. Moreover I had not forgotten that I was not legally equipped to cross any frontiers. I had no papers at all, and was carrying in my suitcase a sum far in excess of that allowed by the regulations.

I turned back along the road to the village, regained the

bush, and consulted my map and compass. Hereabouts the vegetation was not dense; and it seemed at first glance an easy matter to bypass the barrier and cross the frontier elsewhere with the help of the compass. But no one knew better than I did the volume of illicit diamond traffiicking that went over this particular frontier, and how much more strictly than hitherto it was now being patrolled by the forces of law and order – at my own insistence, I reflected a little wryly.

I scanned the sides of the road for telegraph poles and wires. There were none, and I felt sure that the news of my disappearance, even if it had reached Sagresa, would not yet have reached an outpost such as this. Nevertheless, prudence dictated not attempting to make my illicit exit until nightfall. When it came at last, it was a cloudy night, quite different from the preceding one. I had to use matches to read the compass as I turned first southwards on a course parallel with the border, then, after a safe distance, eastwards toward it. I made no attempt to follow paths, but simply made my way slowly through the tall grass and scrubby bushes which covered the area.

I had deliberately chosen this overland sector of the boundary because I wanted to avoid the congestion of the bridge and ferry crossings. But now it seemed to my excited senses that the whole dark landscape was peopled with moving shadows, all jostling each other in their haste to cross the invisible boundary without being detected. The ardent fireflies and glowworms presented themselves to my overstretched imagination as smuggled diamonds glowing in the depths of countless pockets. I am, as I had shown before, normally a timid man; and I will not deny that that night I was thoroughly frightened of being caught by my own police. I suppose I realised the impossibility, once I had been identified, of producing any explanation of my behaviour that would sound even faintly plausible. This thought alarmed me much more than the mere possibility of falling foul of the law for the first time in my life, and suffering its penalties. I remember thinking that if caught, I was much more likely to be judged insane than criminal.

I had just snuffed out a match by whose light I was re-checking my direction, when I realised that, about a hundred yards from me, there was another light burning. This time there could be no mistaking it. It was the old gold of a kerosene lamp flame, not the starry silver of a firefly or glow-worm. And it was moving, slowly, stealthily, directly toward me. From the swing of the light, I could judge the stride of its carrier: a long, careful pace, that of a stalker; of the hunter, not the hunted.

I stood rooted in terror. If I had moved immediately I saw the light, I might have escaped discovery; but now any move I made in that long grass would certainly be heard at the closing distance which separated the advancing light from me. As the first blind rush of terror receded from me, and reason reasserted itself, I could only hope that if the un-known person's advance toward me was a trick of chance and I had not in fact been seen or heard, something would intervene in his path to make him change course before the next few seconds were out.

Exquisitely slowly the gap closed, and still there was no deviation of course. I strained my eyes to catch a glimpse of the person behind the swinging light, but the wick was turned down low, and I could see nothing except a dark, loping silhouette.

Then suddenly, when only a few feet separated us and it seemed almost as if we should collide, the stranger saw me. The look which sprang to his face, and the cry which leapt from his lips remain vivid impressions to this day. The look was one of stark dread, with staring, dilated eyeballs, en-gorged neck muscles, and twitching lips. The cry was that of beast, not of man; a guttural, half-choking sob of terror. As for me, I do not remember feeling any sensation of relief at the discovery that my own fear of what was approaching was so completely out-proportioned by that of the stranger. For a second or two we stood, the lamp still swinging in ever shorter arcs between us, not wishing, or not able, to stir. Then something about his appearance prompted me to say a single word of greeting to him in Hausa. The smile which spread slowly from the bared teeth, yellow in this light, to the sweat-beaded brow, unnaturally furrowed from the same cause, was the smile that members of a family reserve for each other all over the world.

Strange how, without even seeing each other's faces clearly, that man and I found such companionship in each other that night. Partly, perhaps, it was a reaction from our common initial fright; partly the feeling that we both, for different reasons, needed, or might need, a friend before the night was over. I learned from him, as we squatted in the grass, his now extinguished lamp resting on my suitcase, that he was indeed an illicit diamond miner. He was returning from a trip across the border to make a rendezvous with a diamond-buying agent. Something had gone wrong with their plans, and the rendezvous had not taken place. He dared not wait longer at the place arranged, and was returning to his own side of the border, hoping to make his way back ultimately to the mining village where he ran a petrol station as a 'blind'.

I plucked up my courage. Damn it, I was well and truly on the other side of the law now, the confidant of smugglers; so I might as well go the whole hog. 'Brother, you have diamonds now?' I asked in a low voice.

'Yes,' he nodded vigorously. I could just see the teeth and eyeballs moving vertically. Whatever moon there had been had long since set, and there was only starlight.

'Then why keep your lamp lit so the police will see you easily?' I pursued.

He made no reply for a moment, and seemed to be weighing up the arguments for and against telling me more. Finally it was pride in his cleverness, I suppose, that got the better of his caution. Taking my hand, he guided it to the screw cap of the filler hole in the reservoir of the kerosene lamp. It was a large lamp. 'Undo it,' he said, with an unmistakable chuckle in his voice. I did. 'Feel inside.' I thrust a tentative finger into the hole. Within was the longest wick I ever saw, or rather felt. It seemed to coil in endless loops, so that there was hardly room for much kerosene. And at intervals along its length were stitched the stones, some small, some large: not a great number, but still representing a major fortune.

'Policemen do not think of searching a lighted lamp,' he said in my ear, as if one of the victims of his trick were standing over us. 'A lamp that is not lit, yes; they shake it, they open it, they search everywhere. But a lamp that is lit – nobody notices it!'

His fund of stories that night seemed inexhaustible. I must have seemed to him, by comparison, to have led a very ordinary, unexciting sort of life. If all he said was to be believed, he had been at this game for many years now; but had not made very much out of it, as there were too many middlemen involved, of all races and nationalities. But he had a comfortable living, and more material benefits than he had ever dreamed would come his way; so he had no quarrel with any of his numerous principals. I could not, of course, return his confidence. I told him I had had an urgent business call to attend to in a seaport across the border, and not having had time to get my passport visaed for the journey, was risking the illegal route. Then suddenly an idea struck me.

'Do you want to sell those diamonds now?' I asked my new-found friend.

'Certainly. Somehow I am not used to travelling in *this*

direction with a heavy lamp, and I do not feel at ease. That's why I was so frightened when I saw you standing like a tree in front of me just now.'

'I'll buy the heavy lamp from you for – let us say, two hundred and fifty pounds cash down.'

The whites of the eyes increased noticeably in area. 'At once, now?' he asked wonderingly. I thought: those crooks he deals with must have been making a huge profit out of this country bumpkin. Removing the lamp respectfully from the suitcase, I slipped back the straps securing the lid, and snapped back the metal catches. I fumbled around until my fingers touched the newspaper-wrapped package containing the currency notes. Lifting out the package, I undid it carefully on my lap, counted out five of the ten £50 note bundles, and handed them to my brother. I wondered for a moment whether he would even take the precaution of lighting his previous lamp and having a look at what I was giving him in exchange for it. But not to do this was clearly beyond the limits to which brother will trust brother. There was a pause while he listened intently into the silence. Then I heard the click of the lantern glass being raised and the scratch of the match. The little yellow flame entered the glass shade and ignited the wick. In a few seconds a moist forefinger had flicked its way with graceful, practised ease through the bundles. Without further comment, the lamp was extinguished and placed in my hands. Only then did he speak.

'I thank you very much, my brother. No one before has paid me so much so quickly for my diamonds. You are a good brother to me.'

If truth be known, I had acted very much on an impulse. I had no idea of the value of the diamonds, but did have only too vivid a recollection of my fears of being caught with all those notes in my suitcase. I had also been worried about the problem of obtaining foreign exchange for so much

Songhai currency. The trick of the lighted lamp had impressed me at once as almost foolproof; and I felt if I could get that wick across the frontier the wealth it represented might help forward my difficult mission a little further.

'Can I guide you across the border to safety? I know all these parts as if it were my own country.'

'Yes, please,' I answered quickly. 'Light on or off?'

He considered for a moment. 'You have any more money in that suitcase?'

'Yes.'

'A lot?'

'About the same as I have just given you.'

'Better keep the light out, then. The patrols are certain to search that suitcase if they see us. Come on. We must get across before daybreak.' And he jumped up, picked up my suitcase, and set off at his previous pace, slow, measured, relaxed. Queer, now I come to think of it, how I never had even a moment of mistrust about his intentions.

Six hours later I was bidding him good-bye on the outskirts of a small village across the border by the grey light of an early dawn. He was a thick-set fellow with large, friendly eyes. Soon he was loping off the way we had come, and was lost to my sight in the high grass.

With the danger of being searched now behind me, I emptied the kerosene from the lamp, fished out the lower end of the loaded wick, drew it free from the holder, and threw the lamp away. After some searching I found a main road, and a lorry soon appeared to take me to the nearest village. It was a village of only modest size, but I was able to find a householder of my own tribe who was willing to give me a meal and a bed for the night in exchange for sterling. The next day I was on a post office van whose driver I paid exorbitantly to get me to the capital by next morning.

He kept his word; and after a relatively well-sprung

journey I was deposited on the outskirts of a large city. My van driver friend had been only too glad, in exchange for five pounds, to supply information with regards to the illicit diamond market here. A few hours after my arrival, having lunched well in a hotel, I was knocking a little nervously at the unpainted door of a grimy little hovel. More than most African towns, this one was a place of violent contrasts. There were wealthy neighbourhoods cheek by jowl with poverty-stricken ones; well-paved and perfectly constructed streets leading direct into the most wretched potholed tracks, which would suddenly change back again into respectable thoroughfares. I had walked through some parts of the central area which would have done credit to almost any city in the world, with neat blocks of modern flats, well-designed shops and public buildings, and smoothly working public amenities and traffic arrangements.

But the worst parts were still most depressing; and this was one of them. As I waited for the door to open I gazed up and down the street, and everywhere there seemed to be squalor and disorder. It was with a certain relief to counter-balance my nervousness that I saw the door open and a wizened little man look out.

'Good afternoon, sir. I have come to do business.' I lowered my voice. 'Diamonds.'

He gave no sign of surprise, satisfaction, or anything else. The deep sunken eyes gazed at me intently, suspiciously. Then, 'Caame in,' he drawled thickly.

Over a table in a room so full of odd pieces of furniture of every description that it needed considerable effort even to cross it, he peered through a variety of lenses and eye-glasses at every inch of the stone-studded wick, in complete silence. After perhaps five minutes he looked up.

'Fiftee' hundred U.S. dolla,' he said unemotionally.

I stifled a gasp as best I could. 'Did you say "fifty hundred" or "fifteen"? I didn't quite catch you.'

'Ah may be ol, but ah'm sure no crazy yet. Ah said one five nought nought. They're naw worth a cent more.'

I had neither the inclination nor the need, now, to haggle. I had still made a very good bargain.

'I'll take it, if it's cash down.'

He hobbled off immediately, clutching the wick in talon-like fingers. His footsteps creaked up wooden stairs a few seconds later, and shuffled over the floor above.

When I get back to Songhai, the first thing I'll do is find my brother and tell him what a fool he is to stop short at the border and not bring his stones here himself, I thought.

After what seemed a long time, the footsteps creaked down again. The money was in neat bundles of twenty-dollar bills. I checked it carefully, replaced the elastic band which the old man had provided, tucked the money into my suitcase, and then took my leave with as much alacrity as was consistent with courtesy. My host was equally hurried in showing me out. We seemed to be in the unusual position, for a buyer and seller, of being both equally certain that we had secured a fabulous bargain.

I knew that I now had all the money that I needed for the task that lay ahead. I called at a department store and bought a new suitcase, a suit off the peg, and adequate supplies of shirts, socks, and underwear. I washed and changed in a public convenience, and noted with satisfaction from the mirror that, with my faint bristle of hair, dark glasses and three-day-old growth of beard, I looked like a slightly eccentric but well-heeled bum, newly arrived from the bush. I now made my way to the city's best hotel, booked in, and snuggled in happily to the comforts of civilised living once more.

I think I realised that it would be the last time for a considerable period that I should be able to enjoy such comforts. I confess willingly that I have a weakness for civilised living in the Western sense. For one day and one night I let everything slip. I wallowed neck-deep in a piping hot bath for an hour. I ordered certainly the largest dinner that particular waiter had ever brought up to any guest's room, judging from the expression of admiration on his face. After dinner I asked my way to a night club. The atmosphere inside shimmered with brassy jazz, and was criss-crossed thickly with long, low lecherous looks; but I managed to find an agreeable companion and returned to my hotel room with the first streaks of day, just pleasantly drunk.

The next day I had one or two important things to do. First of all I reserved a seat on the plane leaving in two days' time for South Africa, and bought an open round ticket for the journey. Then a call at the Passport Office to get a passport and at the South African Embassy for a visa; and all was now ready for my journey.

I slept deeply and dreamlessly the next two nights, and shook off the combined effects of my earlier night of indulgence and my previous days of strain. Before dawn the third morning a taxi took me to the helicopter station in the centre of the town; and at 5 a.m. we took off for the airport. It was a short flight along the coast, in the cold mistiness of the early morning; and I experienced a curious absence of emotion at the start of the final stage of my journey. I was neither excited nor depressed; but I do remember that at this point once more the realisation that I was acting under the influence of a will stronger than my own was vivid. We skimmed lazily over beaches and palm trees, roads and occasional huts, until the broad expanse of the airfield tarmac came into view to the east. The whirr of the rotor blades changed its note as the pilot altered their pitch and allowed us to fall gently. With the slightest of bumps we were down outside the terminal, and shepherded into the huge silver airliner that stood waiting a few yards away. I was approaching the final irrevocable step in my adventure. There was just time now to make some excuse to myself and to those around and turn back. But I was contemplating the possibility now purely as an academic exercise, weighing up the pros and cons of the matter as if I were in the chair at a debate. I was still trying hard to be strictly impartial when I heard the triumphant cough and roar as one by one the engines fired, and then the gentle voice of the stewardess asked me if I would be so kind as to fasten my seat belt.

The sun was setting in a vast ruddy furnace over the western rim of the Plateau as we circled round and round the airfield at Johnstown, losing height imperceptibly.

Passing high over the legislative capital, I had given an involuntary gasp of admiration at the beautiful symmetry of the Omega-shaped Republican Buildings there. It seemed to me then so natural a thing that a similar balance of proportions should be achieved between the interests of the races of South Africa as had been struck between the architectural elements of this its finest building.

We touched down, and with a surprising lack of formality I was granted permission to enter the Republic of South Africa for three months of 'sight-seeing'.

In fact I knew I had exactly two months in which to find Friedrik before Congress called *apartheid*'s bluff. I began my long search through telephone directories. 'F. Hertogs' were numerous, and I lounged across the street from many front doors in many towns before I found him. I followed him to the door of his club, and next day secured a job in the club's kitchen. Then finally the day came on which I knew I should have to face him. Late that evening I went up to the lounges to clean up. He was very drunk, and did not even recognise me. In a fever of anticipation, I brushed against him as I passed with a brush, and he glared up at me angrily.

'Say, Joe,' he shouted to the manager of the club, 'how many more niggers you going to hire here, eh?'

'Better make use of them while we can, Mr Hertog,' Joe replied soberly.

'We don't agree, do we, boys?' asked Friedrik thickly. 'If they're going to walk out on us one day, why should we be putting bread in their mouths now when it suits them. You've got to fire this nigger, Joe.'

'I need more help, Mr Hertog. Can you get me someone else?'

'We don't care if we have to wash our own dishes. We don't want to see that nigger here tomorrow night, do we, boys?'

There was a murmur of support from the other members of the club. Friedrik drained his glass and ordered another drink. I wiped mud from the floor by the front door. It was raining hard outside, I noticed.

I cleared the tables and finished my chores. It was near midnight, and the lounges were emptying. Friedrik went out last, staggering badly. 'Don't forget what we said, Joe,' he slurred.

But I was already on my way out of the back door, in an agony of frustration. When I reached the front of the building there was no sign of Friedrik. The rain was still falling in sheets. I started off at a run in the direction I knew he must have taken.

When I caught up with him he was weaving across the street in wide serpentine movements. I followed him at a distance of a few paces, relishing the mere knowledge that he was at last completely in my power. Then suddenly he stumbled over a kerb and fell heavily. He lay very still as I stood over him, and as the first drums began to send their throbbing message out across the night it was pity I found in my heart for him, not hate. I stooped quickly, lifted him gently, and bore him through the easing rain to the safety of his home.

can, Mr Herzog,' Joe

asked Friedrik thickly. 'If
one day, why should we be
now when it suits them.
Joe.
Herzog, Can you get me someone

wash our own dishes. We
here tomorrow night, do we

the other members
he glass and ordered another
floor by the front door. It was

aware of my chores. It was near
upsetting Friedrik went
forget what we said, Joe.'

the back door, in an
the front of the build
he rain was still falling
the direction I knew he

weaving across the
followed him at a dis
knowledge that he
Then suddenly he
He lay very still as
one over to send the
it was pity I found
quickly lifted him
ain to the safety